SPUR #23

SAN DIEGO SIRENS

Dirk Fletcher

LEISURE BOOKS   ∞   NEW YORK CITY

Special thanks to Scott Cunningham for his valuable contribution to this book.

A LEISURE BOOK

Published by

Dorchester Publishing Co., Inc.
6 East 39th Street
New York, NY 10016

Printed in the United States of America

STARING DOWN THE MUZZLE OF A SPENCER RIFLE

Spur stood for a split second as the rifle barrel jabbed against his forehead, then shoved his boot hard into the man's groin. The assailant howled in pain as Spur sent his forearm flying through the air. It struck the Spencer, sending it whirling to the floor.

"Jee-suz!"

Spur slammed his hotel room's door shut, drove his fist into the man's bobbing chin, and followed up with a jab at the soft stomach for good measure. Two hundred pounds hit the floor and skidded backwards ten feet.

McCoy jumped onto the man's chest. As Spur reached for his pistol something smashed into his chin, sending him reeling backwards. He nearly lost his balance as the would-be killer scrambled out from between Spur's legs and groped on the floor for the rifle. . . .

Also in the Spur series:

SAN DIEGO SIRENS

1

Sunlight slanted harshly across the Southern California valley, twenty miles from the growing seaport of San Diego. Massive boulders the size of houses festooned the angular, brown mountains, casting lengthening shadows as the afternoon slid toward dusk.

Lazy Eye's deerskin leggings dragged in the dust as he walked through the opened gate onto the ranch ahead. Pride surged through the nineteen year old Indian boy, strengthening the handsome, thin features of his bronzed face. He'd taken the first step toward independence. The cattle were safe, hidden where Bucher would never find them. He'd made a rude pen for them from young tree trunks he'd felled, filled the troughs with water, and piled in cut grass for the beasts to eat. They'd be safe until he could return to care for them.

Early that morning, when the ranch had been quiet, he'd slipped into the barn and stolen ten of the counterfeit gold double-eagles from the saddlebag where his boss had carelessly hidden them. Then, nonchalantly, he'd left the barn by the back door and began the long journey on foot to the Mexican rancher's place. He'd told the man he needed ten head of cattle for his boss. The Mexican eagerly grabbed up the double-eagles and turned over the cows.

Soon he'd be free of his boss, Lazy Eye thought victoriously. Soon he and his sister could live as they wished.

"How's it feel to know you're gonna die?" a guttural, Germanic voice bellowed out.

Lazy Eye turned in surprise to see Emil Bucher, his employer, walking toward him, the shimmering barrel of a Winchester pointed toward his chest. The man cocked it savagely.

"I no . . ." the Indian began, then English failed him. His cheeks flushed.

"Shut the fuck up!" Bucher said, spitting the words as he advanced on the unarmed Indian. "You money hungry *bastard*! You stole from me. You didn't think you could do that and get away with it, did you? You can't. Not with me. Now hold still so I won't waste ammo blowing you into hell."

Lazy Eye started towards the man.

"Don't move! Not another step. I wanna watch you squirm as I blast your stomach to bits!"

Lazy Eye stopped and stared at the red-faced, tall man. He'd be dead soon. He knew it. His boss never pointed a rifle at a man unless he meant to kill him.

Lazy Eye didn't understand everything the man was saying, but he could sense the meaning of the words that Bucher kept screaming at him, wild-eyed. He knew he should do something—attack the man, run, something. But the white man's apparent superiority had him cowered.

"Good-for-nothing Indian!" Bucher said.

"Please." Lazy Eye's chest tightened and his throat constricted. He couldn't stop staring at the rifle.

"No way, *idiot!* I gave you a chance, you bastard. You blew it. I trusted you and you stabbed me in the back. It's too late now."

Panic rose up with him. Save yourself, he thought. Lazy Eye lifted his hands before him. "Mister Bucher," he began. "I did not—"

"I told you to shut up!" Bucher thundered. "Only trouble is, how should I kill you? I could blow out your brains—if you had any." He chuckled, a deep laugh from his belly. "No. A belly shot first, or should I shoot off your legs and arms one at a time? Maybe I'll start with your fingers." The German scratched his side with his elbow. "I gotta think about this."

Lazy Eye had no knife, no gun, no weapons. Bucher had locked up his knife the day Lazy Eye had accidentally wandered into Bucher's place seven months ago, saying something about how he didn't trust any damn Indian with a weapon. Though he had another one back at his camp he knew better than to bring it to the ranch with him.

He'd taken the job Bucher offered him, even though he couldn't come to the ranch armed, and had to sneak back to visit his sister when he could, because he needed the food and supplies the man said he'd give to Lazy Eye in exchange for working.

The Indian's mind flashed to the picture of his sister, Bird Song, at their camp that morning, smiling at him as he left for the ranch. What would happen to her if he was dead? He'd promised their mother to take care of her just before the coughing sickness had sent her spirit to join their grandfather's in the sky.

"Maybe I should shoot off your dick first," Bucher said, and laughed raucously as he watched the man stand helplessly before him. "You bastard! You have to pay. I oughta make you die slow, maybe make you spend a day and night watching your guts fall out of your belly, covered with blood."

"Mister Bucher," Lazy Eye said, "please." Then the English words wouldn't come. Why hadn't he learned from his sister? She always said it would make it easier for him, but he hadn't wanted to speak the language of the strange man who'd massacred his people. Why hadn't he done all the things she'd wanted to do?

Bucher strode to the Indian and slammed the Winchester's butt into the man's neck. Lazy Eye spun onto the dirt. Bucher bashed the young man's spine, pounding the rifle's stock into the delicate area, as Lazy Eye moaned and twisted on the ground. "Fuckin' Indian!"

As pain screamed through his body, running like boiling water in his veins, the youth at first tried to block it. When he couldn't he fed on it, funneling the agony into his self-defense mechanisms. The Indian kicked the Winchester from Bucher's hands, then squatted, feeding off the pain that roared through his body. Blood poured out of his neck from an opened cut, his heart pumping it out in spurts to slide down along his bare, well-tanned torso.

"You bastard!" Bucher said.

Lazy Eye felt his knees weaken as Bucher scrambled over to the gun. The pain increased tenfold as his legs lost all feelings and went numb. He stumbled for balance, never moving his gaze from the German.

"You think you're smart, don't you?" Bucher said, hefting the rifle up before the defenseless boy. "You're not. I am."

Kick the rifle away, Lazy Eye told himself. Kick the rifle away! He tightened his right leg's thigh muscles, then shifted his weight. The ground slammed up against his cheek, dazing him. His spine spasmed uncontrollably; his legs were limp, useless, damaged beyond repair.

"Holy mother, what in hell's goin' on, Bucher?" a voice drawled.

"Shut up, Shorty!" Bucher yelled as a five foot six man ran up. "Just teaching this damn devil a lesson he'll never forget, not even when he's dead."

Shorty smiled as he walked up, arms folded

11

across his broad chest. "What's Lazy Dick done now? Gotten a piece off your squaw?" He snorted as he stood looking down at the Indian lying on the ground. Lazy Eye's bare back lay open, the skin slashed, oozing blood.

"He stole some of the goddamned double-eagles!" Bucher said. "Probably went into town to get some white woman. I'm just figuring how to kill him."

"Why not let me?" The short man's face brightened. "C'mon, Bucher! You never let me have any fun. I'll kill him right quick for you."

"Shut up and get back to work!" the man yelled, gesturing with the Winchester. "I'll handle this. By the time you're done making those ten blanks this bastard will be dead. Get your ass back out here and plant him in the ground somewhere so he won't be found."

"Sure, boss," Shorty said.

"Get moving!"

Shorty ambled away toward the barn, staring at the men over his shoulder, frowning.

Lazy Eye glared up at the white man before him. He had no sensation below the waist; he was paralyzed, helpless. The young man struggled not to show the fire that sizzled through his backbone.

"Git ready to slide into hell." Bucher pushed the rifle's muzzle against Lazy Eye's left temple. "Like the feeling of that? That's your death, boy."

The Indian stared at him, the corners of his mouth tight, lips pressed together.

"You'll never steal from me again!" Bucher roared and pulled the trigger.

The Indian's head exploded into a mass of blood-covered chunks of flesh and bone mixed with singed black hair. His lifeless body flopped onto the ground and lay still.

Bucher's laugh crackled through the valley, mixing with the last of the rifle's thunder, until both were lost on the updrafts of the strong, hot, ceaseless wind.

Don Arturo Guerra slapped the gold coins onto the rubbed wood desk as he strode into the marshal's office. "Counterfeit," he said.

Wallace Weschcke, Caliente's town marshal, picked up one of the coins, frowned, then took a pearl-handled throwing knife from his desk and scratched a deep line on the double-eagle with the blade. A thin layer of gold easily peeled off the coin, revealing a dull metallic core. "I'll be damned," the full-bodied man said.

"I should have checked them. I thought it was too good to be true," Guerra said, "selling ten good-for-nothing cows to that Indian for two hundred American dollars. That *Indio* said it was for his boss." He spat at the brass bowl on the dusty floor beside Weschcke's desk.

"Counterfeit coins? Here in Caliente?" Weschcke ran his fingers through his full, white beard. "I can't believe it." He eyed the coins, then glanced up at Guerra.

"Believe it, Marshal. I believe I'm out ten head, two hundred dollars," the stocky Mexican man said in perfect but accented English.

Weschcke grunted. "Something like this can ruin your whole day," he mumbled. "Wonder if any more've showed up in town. I'll have to check."

"What are you going to do about this?" Guerra demanded.

"Said you got it from an Indian?"

Guerra nodded. "A young brave. He walked onto my ranch this morning."

"I'll send a man to check for Indians, but without a good description I don't think we'll ever find the buck who cheated you."

"Do something!" Guerra said.

"Calm down, Don Arturo," Weschcke said gently. "Could have happened to anyone."

"I know, but it happened to me. Do whatever you can. *Estupido*. It's my own stupidity that got me into this mess, but do what you can." He turned and stormed out of the room.

Louella Bucher stood before the full length mirror as she reached behind her, buttoning up her black and red, tightly waisted dress. She admired the curves of her body, the swelling breasts, naturally slim waist, and flaring hips.

Even though she knew she wouldn't be seeing her father for several days, she wanted to look her best on the train ride to San Francisco, before she started the long stage coach trip to Caliente, California, wherever that was.

Besides, Louella thought, maybe some man on the train would like what he saw, take her to an empty compartment, and make her feel like a woman.

She touched her neck, then trailed her hand down to cup her large, firm breasts.

She shook her head. Stop it, Louella, she told herself firmly, and dropped her hands to her sides. That's behind you now. The hungry look in her eyes faded as she stared into her reflection.

She was traveling to join her father and start a new life. Philadelphia bored her now. The operas, the teas, the endless social activities that her aging Aunt Agnes forced her into attending had nearly driven her mad. Even the handsome men who so gladly dropped their drawers and gave her what she wanted had begun to lose their charm, so she'd decided to go to California, where if nothing else there were ten thousand men to each woman. That should keep her busy.

No. Not anymore, Louella reminded herself, as she continued to admire her reflection. She'd be a good little girl to her father, even though she was twenty-five. Still unmarried, Louella knew no one man could ever satisfy her. It was becoming more difficult to hide her nightly activities with the fine young gentlemen of Philadelphia from her maiden aunt. But in California—well, maybe she could manage to settle down for a while. It might be a nice change.

Her mother had been killed six years ago by a stray bullet during a holdup on the morning train. Louise Bucher's demise had changed her father. He'd begun to drink, stopped attending church and had sent his daughter to live with his sister in

Philadelphia when he'd left for California.

Her mother's death had shocked Louella into realizing that there was more to life than dressing properly or lifting her little finger when she drank her tea. She hadn't been living, just spending her time waiting for a man to marry her and take her virginity.

A few months after her mother's death she'd found a man, a young lawyer, but marriage wasn't on his mind. After looking around for a suitable husband she finally began enjoying all the sinful things she'd always secretly wanted.

Louella sighed as she tied a simple bonnet around her chin. Perfect, she decided. When she walked onto her father's ranch, unannounced, he'd be proud of her. And apparently he was doing well; the last letter she'd received six months ago said the ranch was prospering.

Louella lifted her traveling bags and, straining under their weight, left her aunt's house for the last time and walked to the train station. She hadn't had the heart to tell her aunt that she was leaving, knowing the screaming argument they'd have, while her Aunt Agnes threw her hand to her heart and pretended another attack. No. Louella would send a telegram sometime during the journey.

Standing, waiting for the 8:05 train, she wondered if she was doing the right thing. California was a long way away, and Caliente— she'd never heard of it before her father's first telegram. The old fears of the unknown rattled through her for a second as she stood poised, ready to turn back, unpack her bags, and smile as her aunt walked into the house.

Louella shook off her doubts. Her father would be happy to see her, she told herself firmly. It had been six years. And she was sure Caliente was a wonderful town.

Besides, anything would be better than stuffy Philadelphia.

When he'd finished striking the last of the ten blanks in the barn Shorty stacked them up on the rickety table next to the stove where he melted the base metals, ready for Bucher to coat them with gold. He wiped the gritty sweat from his forehead, then smiled and walked out to find the dead Indian.

What a mess, Shorty thought, staring down at the bloodied, slashed body. Too bad he couldn't have done it. That damn Bucher knew how much he enjoyed killing but never let him have his fun. Nothing he could do about it now.

He bent and dragged the body to the far side of the barn, got the rusty shovel and put his back into the work.

Thirty minutes later Shorty threw the body into the shallow grave, kicked some dirt over it, and wiped his slick forehead. Good enough burial for that asshole he thought. When he'd completely covered the body he looked down at it, shrugged, and walked back to the bunkhouse. He needed a whiskey.

Goddamn Bucher never let him have any fun!

2

Spur McCoy slammed down behind the San Francisco bar as the huge plate glass mirror exploded overhead, raining glass onto the floor.

"You're as good as dead," a large man with a tin star on his chest shouted from the other side of the bar. "Fuckin' around with my Missy. I told you time and again to keep your hands offa my daughter! Now you're gonna die for that roll in the hay last night, you goddamned bastard!"

Great, Spur thought. All he'd wanted was a quick drink to help him sleep before he went to the station, and he'd gotten involved in some petty local dispute.

"Go ahead and shoot him, Sheriff!" a gruff voice called out from the saloon. "He always did water the whiskey!"

"Yeah!" another drunk said. "He ain't worth more'n day old piss!"

"Stay outa this," the sheriff warned.

"I never touched her," a thin, moustached man said, squatting ten feet from Spur behind the bar.

"Like hell!"

"She'll tell you. We just went walkin' in the moonlight last night after the dance. Honest! I'd never do nothin' to Missy, Sheriff! Why would I, since you come in here everyday threatening to blow my balls off if I so much as look at her sideways? Ask her!"

"I don't have to," the man growled. "I looked at her dress when she came in last night. Blood all over it—cherry blood. You touched her all right, you bastard! Inside. Outside. Shit, Ferris, you've made her good for nothin' but whoring. No man'll marry her now. Get on yer goddamned legs so I can lock you up, give you a fair trial, then watch you kick off at the end of a rope! I wanna hear your neck *snap*, Ferris, you goddamned coward! You deserve it after messin' around with my Missy!"

Christ, thought Spur, shrugging off the glass shards from his hat and caot. He didn't have time for this.

"I said stand up!" the sheriff bellowed. "If I have to shoot you here and now I will!"

"Might as well get it over with," Spur said to the luckless bartender. "He's a lawman. He'll never kill you here in front of all these witnesses."

The man glanced at him, trembling. "You don't know him. When it comes to his Missy that man plumb loses his senses." He wiped his hands on the front of his stained apron, then frowned, eyes wild, jerking left and right. "Shit."

"C'mon, Ferris, do it!" some drinker yelled.

"Yeah, give us a little show!"

McCoy thought of the telegram in his pocket. Damn! He had about five minutes to make the next train down to Los Angeles, and no time for this. He poked his head above the bar. The sheriff stood five feet away, and he wasn't smiling. Just as Spur started to rise to his feet the bartender piped up.

"Sheriff, I—" the barkeep started.

The big man's .44 sounded again, shattering a row of whiskey bottles and a crate of beer. Liquid soaked glass again pounded the floor behind the bar. Spur ducked against its onslaught and felt the shards bouncing off his hat.

"Maybe hangin's too good for you, Ferris!" the sheriff said. "Maybe I ought to serve justice right here and now. Hell, I know you're guilty. No reason to bother the judge about this. I'll be your judge and jury!"

Make up your mind, Spur thought as he crouched behind the bar again. He had to move. McCoy scrambled out past the end of the long bar and collided with a table, spilling a half played game of checkers to the floor. He grabbed his traveling bag from a hook near the door and ran from the saloon.

McCoy blew out his breath as the cool evening fog outside wrapped around him. No reason to get involved in that mess, he thought, as a gunshot thundered out from the saloon. Spur hurried his steps. He hadn't had much rest in San Francisco, and now it was back to work.

Caliente, California, McCoy thought as he lit a cheroot with a sulphur match and walked briskly toward the station, his boots clicking on the wooden boardwalk. Never heard of it, but the wire'd said the town was twenty miles from San Diego.

According to the assignment, someone was counterfeiting U.S. currency in Caliente, or at least an Indian had passed some fake double-eagles to a rancher near the settlement. The town marshal was worried that more of the bogus coins would show up, might even spread to San Diego, though he'd checked—they hadn't. Yet.

Spur sighed and puffed the cheroot. He had a long trip ahead of him.

Ten minutes later the six foot two, tightly packed two hundred pound man leaned against his seat on the train and tried to sleep. An agent of the Secret Service, Spur was heading toward a case that reminded him of the agency's original intent—to investigate, halt and bring to justice criminals who were broke enough, dumb enough or desperate enough to try to counterfeit U.S. currency. It'd been a long time since he'd been assigned a case like this.

He needed a holiday and a woman, Spur thought, then drowsed as steam shot up from the engine and the wood burning train slowly rattled away from the city by the bay.

An hour later he woke. His eyes focused on a beautiful middle-aged woman who sat nervously in the seat across from him. She crossed her legs tightly and her hand rose from her lap to clasp her breast as his eyes met hers.

"Oh, I'm sorry," she said. "I wasn't really staring at you." The woman lowered her gaze.

"I'm not complaining," Spur said.

She smiled nervously, like a kid who'd been caught stealing a cracker from a general store's barrel. "I moved to this car because all the others were full, and I-I—"

As she blushed Spur thought how much more attractive it made her. She's hot blooded, Spur thought, feeling a stirring in his groin. Down boy. He shifted his legs to compensate for his arousal as the woman continued to gape at him, obviously embarrassed at having been caught looking at him.

Sleep, he told himself. "If you'll pardon me," Spur said as he tipped his hat down over his face.

"Of course." She smiled sweetly, relieved.

As Spur started to drowse he saw the woman's gaze travel down to his crotch, then saw nothing at all.

The dusty screen door banged behind him as Emil Bucher stormed into the ranch house's kitchen an hour's ride from Caliente. He was hungry. Where was that squaw?

Beef stew simmered in the enameled pot on the stove, and a loaf of freshly baked bread lay on the cutting board. He tore off one end of the bread, stuffed it into his mouth, then chewed as he walked to the stove. The rich, meaty aroma made his stomach growl. "Squaw!" he yelled.

When she didn't answer he cursed, yanked up a full ladle and poured the steaming stew into his mouth. It burned his lips and tongue. "Damn!" he said, swallowing. Indians, Bucher thought. Never trust them to do a goddamned day's work when you turn your back on them.

He remembered Lazy Eye and the veins on his neck stood out. Goddamn Indian! Sure, he killed the sonofabitch, but fear kicked around in his gut. If the brave had spent those double-eagles in Caliente there could be trouble. Suppose the town marshal got interested and traced Lazy Eye to his ranch. It might endanger his whole operation, deprive him of his richly deserved fortune, and land him in jail—or worse. Damn him! At least the red-skinned devil was where he belonged—under the dirt. He couldn't cause any more problems.

Emil Bucher, forty-nine, was struggling to make his fortune. Of German stock, the pudgy, single minded man had moved to Caliente from a small town outside of Philadelphia, Pennsylvania, thinking to make his fortune in gold. He hadn't, but luck had slipped into his pocket.

Bucher ran his fingers through his coarse, crudely cut black hair and lifted another ladle of stew, waiting for it to cool before he slurped it up through his burnt lips.

Twelve months ago, after five years of traveling the length and breadth of the huge state of California, prospecting all day, every day, he'd heard rumors about caves in the mountains beyond San Diego where free gold fell into your hands. His source had never been able to find the caves, but Bucher was determined. He'd taken the next train south.

The night Bucher got into town, after a bone-bouncing stage coach ride, he spent two dollars in a plush whorehouse in the Stingaree district of San Diego to celebrate his new venture.

A grizzled man had barged into the room while he was enjoying a plump, aging whore, yelling that he'd waited a goddamned half hour and wasn't gonna wait another goddamned minute.

The two men and the whore argued, then came to an agreement. Soon they were both enjoying her, one at each end, and got to talking in between gasps and shit-holy-Jesus's. An hour later at the bar the man offered to sell him two perfect double-eagle dies that he'd bought from a gang who'd hit a shipment heading to the mint in San Francisco.

Bucher saw the dies in the stranger's hotel that night. It wasn't more than fifteen minutes later that he handed over half of his modest Eastern savings to buy them. Maybe even if he didn't strike it rich he could still make a fortune. A plan formed in his mind.

He decided Caliente was the closest town to the supposed gold rich area, so he put money down on an abandoned ranch an hour's ride away. Two months of solitary, back breaking work produced nothing.

But one morning his pickaxe struck quartz crystal geodes, and soon afterwards he opened a vein of free gold. Not a huge one, but enough for his purposes.

Perfect, Bucher thought. No smelting or involved processing, just melt it and use it. During the day he'd experimented mixing different base metals, searching for the formula that simulated real gold's heaviness. He finally found it and started molding blanks, striking them with the dies, coating them with gold and restriking to make perfect imitations of the actual twenty dollar coins.

The results were excellent, but the process was too time consuming to do by himself. So he'd hired three men to help him out—Shorty Palmer, a sometime gunfighter, horse thief and petty bankrobber; Sam Johnson, a hard working black with no apparent past, and Lazy Eye.

Bucher scowled as he thought again of the Indian. Bastard! He'd risked his whole operation, everything he'd worked for, for the past twelve months. Never should have hired him in the first place, Bucher thought. Always had an idea he'd be trouble.

Still, he'd worked hard and had double struck 1500 useable twenty dollar gold pieces so far, with a face value of $30,000. But Bucher was smart. He wasn't about to spend them—he might be caught. When he had made enough he'd go to a big city, sell them to some sucker, and run with the real money.

Bucher felt he had $6,000 worth so far. When he'd made enough of the coins to bring him $50,000 he'd retire. Maybe send some money to his daughter in Philadelphia and have her come to live with him.

Louella. The man thought of his daughter as he'd last seen her six years ago—young, far too pretty for her age, trusting. Then he closed his eyes and rubbed a grimy hand over his face until the image dissolved.

He knew he hadn't done right by her, sending her off to his sister's while he roamed the West looking for his fortune. It'd been hard since his wife had been killed on the morning train by a bullet intended for the conductor. But he knew that someday he'd make it up to her. Someday.

"Squaw!" he yelled again, then stormed from the kitchen and into the parlor. Out the window he saw the woman rising from a squat over a pail. She pressed her black skirt down around her legs as she walked toward him, hips gently swaying.

"Git on in here!" he shouted.

She ran into the ranchhouse then and stood looking up at him with black, knowing eyes. "I come," she said, and turned toward the kitchen.

Bucher grabbed her arm and turned the woman to him. "I don't want food," he said, releasing her. The man lowered his pants, stuffed his hand into his shorts and pulled out his limp penis. He gripped it. "Get to work," he said harshly, pushing her to her knees before him.

"You want?" she asked.

"Yeah, I want," Bucher's voice was sarcastic. "Shut up and eat."

As her warm mouth wrapped around his manhood Bucher knew it was useless. Everytime he thought about his daughter, about his dead wife, he couldn't get excited.

The Germanic man slapped her cheek and

pulled out. "You're not trying," he spat.

As the woman worked him over, tears spilling from her dark eyes, Bucher sighed. He knew he was risking twenty years in a federal prison for counterfeiting, but he was sure he'd set up such a dense smoke screen that no one would be able to penetrate it. Everyone in Caliente thought he was a lazy, good-for-nothing rancher who liked squaws, and he'd never done anything to correct them. No one had a clue as to what he was really doing, and he hadn't exactly run up and down the tiny town's one street banging a drum and saying he'd found gold on his property.

"Suck harder."

The woman redoubled her efforts. Bucher felt blood flow into his groin, stiffening him inside her.

He smiled as the old feelings boiled up inside him. Fuck Lazy Eye, fuck the ranch, fuck everything! Especially this willing, fairly pretty woman whose mouth suctioned him expertly. She'd learned fast and really enjoyed it.

"On your back," he said, yanking it out again.

The squaw smirked and dropped to the floor, then raised her skirt.

Bucher's mouth watered as he stared down at her.

In the dilapidated barn on Bucher's ranch, Sam Johnson poured the molten metal into the blank molds, tipping up the long-handled ladle at precisely the right moment. He'd had enough practice to allow just enough metal to spill into the mold.

The black man set the ladle back on the small stove and wiped his lips. Fool, he told himself. You're a fool. Why don't you just kill that bastard Bucher next time you see him, steal as many of the fake coins as you can carry, and hightail it out of there?

He allowed himself the luxury of the thought for a few minutes, then sighed as he waited for the metal to cool, ready to take the die's impression. Hell, Shorty'd kill me before I rode ten yards from this place, Johnson thought.

No way out. Shit, he'd be thre until Bucher paid him the thousand dollars he'd promised him. Then he'd be free to leave Caliente for good.

No way out. Shit, he'd be there until Bucher paid he wanted. Bucher'd made it clear to both him and Shorty that if they left the ranch—without his strict permission—they'd lose their jobs and their eventual payoffs.

That was more money than Johnson could make in three years of hard work, and for about twelve months or so.

Johnson sighed and quickly rolled a smoke from his bag of makings. This sure beat his last job, shoveling horseshit all day, every day for a dollar a week, he told himself. A man couldn't hardly live on less than a dollar a day. At least he had a place to stay, food to eat, and a day off once in a while—though he couldn't leave the ranch.

He lit the paper cylinder and inhaled the cigarette, bitter tobacco clinging to his teeth. Yeah, count your blessings, man, Johnson thought, and then looked down at the molds.

Shit!

The molten metal had bubbled. Must've poured too quickly.

He'd have to start over.

3

Spur McCoy took the train as far as Los Angeles, then switched to the stage coach to make the final 140-mile jaunt down to San Diego. He'd lost track of the number of Franciscan missions he either saw or heard about from his talkative companions on the journey. They'd been built by Spaniards who preached to the devilish Indians. at least those who hadn't been slaughtered by the Mexicans or the Americans. Spur wondered if they hadn't been better off with their former beliefs.

He arrived in San Diego with a sore back from the stage coach. McCoy ate a satisfying meal a block from the courthouse, then spent the night in a comfortable hotel room on the second floor, as was his practice, where he could keep an eye on things outside. The night passed uneventfully.

The next morning Spur rented a horse and rode

east out of town, passing yet another mission on the cliffs above him as he passed single family Indian camps in the huge valley that stretched to the marshy San Diego Bay. The smoke from the many fires hung in a haze above the broad depression.

For some time he followed a creek, the San Diego River the map called it, though it was nearly dry. The land was desert-like, or semi-desert—few trees, just chapparel and scrub. The air was dry, blowing, and hot.

He found it easily enough. God-forsaken place, Spur thought as he rode into Caliente. The town consisted of three blocks of cleared but rocky ground bordered on each side by widely separated two and three story clapboard buildings. There was a hotel with a saloon and a barber's shop downstairs, a combination mortuary/general store/notary public/post office, a sawbones, and a blacksmith who also ran the town's livery stable. Sixteen houses of dubious construction sat haphazardly between them.

Caliente was an accident. Fifteen years earlier a land speculator who'd made his fortune in San Diego's big land boom had bought up several lots of former grazing land, thinking the railroad might go through there some day.

It never had, but since the town lay on a long trail to Tucson, folks started buying in, putting up houses, opening businesses and buying up the abandoned ranches surrounding the area.

So he eventually created his own little town. He called it Caliente after the Spanish word for hot, an apt title.

Spur turned toward the building marked "Marshal's Office." Kicking through the yellowed, crumpled newspapers that had collected on the sagging front porch Spur walked inside.

A full-bodied man dressed in a three piece suit, with a full white beard and a crown of shoulder length hair, looked up at him in surprise from the paperwork on his desk.

"Weschcke?" Spur asked the man.

"That's right. Wallace Weschcke," the man said in a deeply resonant voice. He moved his chair back and got to his feet. "Help you?" he asked, friendly-like.

"No, I hope I can help you. My name's McCoy."

He shook his head. "I beg your pardon?"

"McCoy, Spur McCoy, from the Secret Service."

He broke into a wide smile. "Mighty happy to meet you, sir, mighty happy!" He extended a hand. "Sorry; I didn't know your name."

Spur shook it. "No reason why you should, I guess. Hear you're having a problem with counterfeit money."

"Some. None's turned up lately; it's been three weeks since Arturo—that's Arturo Guerra—got ten of them from an Indian boy in exchange for some of the sorriest cattle you've ever done seen." Weschcke scratched his chin. "I'm not exactly sure who robbed who."

Spur laughed. "Can I see one of these coins?"

Weschcke opened his desk drawer. "Sure. Have one right here." He flipped it to Spur.

McCoy turned over the double-eagle, examining it. It was counterfeit; even if he hadn't seen the gray metal behind the gold veener that had been scratched off, his instinct told him the coin was the wrong weight.

"We've been watching for more in town. I informed all the merchants, but no more have turned up." Weschcke guffawed. "Hell, every time one of these buggers shows up I'm called in to make sure it's the real McCoy." He looked up at Spur, smiling at the use of the man's surname. "No offense intended, sir."

"None taken," Spur said easily.

"Good."

"Tell me about this Guerra," Spur said, pulling a chair up to the desk. He turned it around and settled down on it as he leaned his wrists against the back.

"Not much to tell. Mexican, about forty, two beautiful young daughters. He's had a ranch in the area for years. Guerra isn't getting rich making money selling cattle around here. He has to drive them up to Los Angeles to sell them."

"Is he an honest man?" Spur asked, wondering how much help the congenial town marshal would be.

Weschcke nodded vigorously. "I'd say so. No problems with him. You can trust Guerra."

"What about the Indian that passed the coins to him? What do you know?"

"Nothing to go on," Weschcke said, and sighed. "All I know is that he's a young Indian man. Don't know what tribe he's from, and no one

I've talked to can give us any help. Seems either he's never been in town, or he has and fits the description of dozens of young bucks that wander in once in a while to buy supplies, whiskey, or women."

Spur raised an eyebrow. "That's a surprise. A town this small's got a sportin' house."

"Not too fancy, but yes, Laurel runs a clean little 'stablishment. She also owns the bar. Most of her ladies came up from San Diego, where there's a hell of a lot more competition. We may be a small town but we get folks passing through on their way to Phoenix, Tucson, Tombstone and other points East."

"I see." Spur'd remember that in case he needed feminine company. "What about the cattle? None with Guerra's brand have showed up where they're not supposed to, have they?"

"Nope. First thing I checked. There's three ranches in the area, well, two real ranches and a third that's—a failure, as I see it."

"And the Indian camps? No luck there, I suppose."

"None. Had to ride nearly all day to reach the first one. I talked with Inaja Cosmit, San Pasqual and the Los Coyotes Indians—they're fairly friendly, considering we've killed most of their kind, then pushed them into the least comfortable lands around these parts, but they weren't any help." He pushed a piece of paper toward Spur. "I've made up a rough map of the area. Thought it might be useful."

Spur took the map and looked it over. Caliente

was the dot in the middle. The three ranches were stars, neatly spaced in the outlying hills, and the three major Indian reservations were marked with circles farther out into the surrounding countryside. Weschcke had crudely drawn in major landmarks.

"What else can you tell me?" Spur asked.

"That's about it." Weschcke clasped his hands on the desk. "Best of luck, Spur. I'll help you any way I can in your 'vestigation. But I've done everything I could think of and still haven't come up with a damn thing."

"Thanks." He rose and turned to the door, folding the map and stuffing it into his pants pocket. "You'll be hearing from me."

He walked out of the marshal's office. This wasn't going to be easy, but few of his cases were.

The rows of foot high grape plants stretched for four square acres, their dark green leaves wilting in the heat of the afternoon sun. Don Arturo Guerra walked to them to check for pests, but quickly realized the grapes were drying out. There wasn't enough water to grow them.

He cursed mildly and went back to his adobe ranchhouse. He'd have to get more water to them, maybe divert the small stream that snaked a half mile from the fields. If he could continue to eke out a little extra cash from the crop he'd be happy. Wine always sold well. Some of the missions grew grapes, he knew, but they were closer to the ocean, as well as to more reliable, accessible water sources.

Don Arturo's *Rancho Hermosa* spread for a hundred acres, the closest point of which was only seven miles from Caliente. His comfortable paunch, easy smile and expensive clothing attested to Guerra's partial success with the ranch, but it wasn't enough. He wanted more.

He'd come a long way from Mexico. Born in Mexico City to poor parents of almost pure Spanish stock, Guerra quickly gained money, power and prestige in the ancient but growing city, rising from a ten year old boy who swept the well treaded floors of an old *cantina* to being the sole owner of the property. When the owner died unexpectedly he left the whole place to him. "The only human being on earth I can trust," the will had said.

Guerra eventually married a woman named Carmella, had twin daughters with fine, silky blonde hair (surely a miracle from God, Guerra had thought when he first saw them) and moved to Guadalajara where he'd amassed more money. After a few years he finally moved up over the border and settled in Caliente, thinking it would grow as San Diego had.

It hadn't, but he was doing well enough, selling cattle once a year to a man in Los Angeles who shipped them up to the big stockyards in San Francisco, as well as a few hundred bottles of wine every year.

As Guerra walked into his *casa* he thought back to the days when he'd strained over a splintery broom, dreaming of living in a big *rancho* with as much food and drink as he wanted. At least he'd realized that dream long ago.

"Concha! Lupe!" he called out into the house. His daughters were the biggest joys in his life—and the biggest pains. He'd been able to hire good men to tend the ranch, so he was free to spend much time with his girls every day.

He sighed as he thought of how quickly Lupe and Concha had taken to the opposite sex once they'd discovered what men and women do together behind closed doors. He knew they slept around—with Spaniards, *gringos,* even Indians at least once, though he'd put a stop to that.

Guerra knew they'd eventually settle down, but he didn't deny them their fun while they were young and adventurous. How could he make them conform to strict moral values when he had courted their mother, Carmella, with one hand on his heart, pledging his love for her, while the other urged her bobbing head faster and faster at his crotch? He smiled at the memory, then called to his daughters again.

Guerra remembered when he was that age. Even at eleven he hadn't any problems finding girls who wanted it as much as he had.

The Mexican pulled on one end of his drooping, coal black moustache and fingered the silver sacred heart medallion that was forever fastened around his neck. God must be pleased with him, Arturo thought, and then turned toward the stairs. "Lupe! Concha!"

No answer. He climbed the stairs, huffing as his extra weight made the journey a chore.

Guerra found the girls in Lupe's bedroom.

Concha was lacing up Lupe's corset as the girl leaned forward, strain showing on her beautiful face.

"Girls, I've been calling you," Guerra said in Spanish as he walked into the room.

"Sorry, Father," Concha said. "We're busy."

"Yes, I can see that."

The twin nineteen year old girls were beautiful, Guerra decided for the thousandth time. They stood before him in corsets, bloomers and silk stockings. Two satin dresses, one virginal white, the other shocking red, lay neatly on the huge goosedown mattress. Concha's hair was pinned up with a tortoise shell comb.

"We're almost dressed," Lupe said. "Just give us a few minutes."

"I'll give you a few minutes, but those two fine men I told you about should be riding up at any minute. Be downstairs to greet them," he gently warned.

"We'll hurry."

Guerra grunted and left the room. That taken care of, he had to check the ledger.

"Tight enough!" Lupe said in Spanish, and bulged out her cheeks outrageously. "Tie it off!"

"All right, Lupe," Concha said, "if you don't want to look your best for your future husband." She finished the knot.

Lupe wrenched free from Concho's grip and shook her head, spilling her glowing blonde hair down around her cheeks. "Husbands. Hah! Probably two old, fat, smelly Spaniards who smoke cigars and think sex means holding hands until after you're married."

"Lupe!" Concha said, glancing at the door as she rushed to the bed. She lifted the dress, dropped it to the floor, and stepped into it. "You know how hard father's trying to find us men."

Lupe smirked, stretching, adjusting to the constriction of the corset. She breathed shallowly so that the movement wouldn't send her into paroxysms of pain as the garment of torture squeezed together her lungs and internal organs. "I don't have any trouble finding men, Concha, and neither do you."

"You know what I mean, Lupe. We're already nineteen. We have to be married soon or—"

"Married to some *hombre* who'll get tired of us after a month and find some other girl." Lupe laughed. She pulled up the dress and pushed her arms into the sleeves. "Is that what you really want, Concha?"

Her sister nodded.

"Do what you want; I'm in no hurry."

Concha frowned, then walked to retrieve her own dress. "Just hurry. We want to make father proud."

"Should I think of father when his friend lays on top of me tonight?"

"Lupe!"

"All right, you win," the whiskey chugging gambler said as he pushed his chair back from the saloon table.

"Twenty dollars," Spur said, gathering up his cards. He'd stopped for a friendly game of poker in Caliente's only saloon and had earned more in one hour than most men made in a week.

"That's a lot of money, mister," the gambler said as he stuffed his hands into his pockets.

"Shouldn't have bet it if you didn't want to lose it." McCoy counted up the pot on the table. "You need three dollars more."

"I know I have it somewhere here," he said, and reached toward the vest pocket beneath his coat.

Spur looked up as the man drew a .44 from his shoulder vest and leveled it at Spur's chest. "I got yer three dollars," he said, and spat tobacco juice onto the table.

4

Spur frowned. "Nothing to get excited about," he said, seated at the saloon table as he tried to talk the young gambler into putting away his drawn gun. Under the saloon table, McCoy's right hand crept along his thigh up to the holster, then held it there.

"I—I know," the young man said. "But that twenty dollars is my eatin' money. I'm supposed to buy beans, bacon, canned peaches—all kinds of shit. Now I went an' lost it in this damn lousy game. My woman's gonna kill me when I git back home!"

"Do you have the three dollars?" Spur asked casually, as he gripped the Colt's handle. He screeched his chair legs to cover the sound of the safety snapping off.

"Sure, I got the three dollars," the man said, his aim dropping somewhat. He looked around the table confusedly.

"Then holster your gun, put the money on the table, and let's just end this game peacefully." Spur slowly drew his weapon, then laid it on his right thigh, ready to use. His finger touched the trigger, waiting.

The gambler hesitated two seconds. Just as Spur was ready to send a bullet plunging into the man's right arm the gambler laid his pistol on the table.

"Good boy," Spur said, and silently holstered his own weapon.

"No hard feelin's, mister, but my wife's gonna leave me when I see her again. She tole me so the last time I did this." He frowned unhappily. "Guess I'm a single man. Shit, I never should've played this game."

"No one twisted your arm," Spur said.

The gambler pulled a dusty gold coin from his pocket and laid it on the table. "Twenty dollars," he said, and collected the seventeen in coins and few bills.

When Spur saw the double-eagle he tensed. Picking it up, he weighed it in his mind. Seemed a bit light. He held it up to catch the light of the wagon wheel style candelabra above him. Looked good, but he couldn't be too careful. Hmmm.

Spur drew his Bowie knife from it's sheath and scraped the suspect coin. Nothing but gold as deep as he scratched.

Seeing Spur's actions, the gambler's face fell. "Shit, you don't trust me, do you, mister?"

"Would you trust a man who'd just pulled a

gun on you, even if he didn't use it?"

"I guess not."

"Besides, heard there was some trouble with counterfeit twenty dollar gold pieces around here. A man can't be too careful."

"My wife—"

"Get home," Spur said. "Before I decide to get mad." Spur showed the man his teeth.

"Yes—yes sir." The youth bolted for the door.

McCoy smiled and pushed the double-eagle into his pocket. So much for peaceful Caliente—and possible leads on the counterfeits. Hell. If nothing else, at least he could afford a bath now.

I'm not sorry I did it, Louella Bucher thought as she stood nude in front of the mirror, her body glowing in the soft kerosene lamplight. The young woman finished washing herself at the porcelain pitcher and basin, then turned the lamp's flame higher and looked behind her. A bearded middle-aged man rubbed his tanned, lean legs and chest as he rose naked from the bed. He grinned, satiated.

Louella hadn't been able to control herself that evening when the handsome man had sat at her table in the San Diego restaurant. He ordered his meal and immediately started telling her his problems. His wife had left him for another man half his age, then he'd lost his job as a fisherman.

As she gazed at his nude body, Louella remembered thinking how'd she feel "guilty" if she left him crying over his mashed potatoes and fried fish while she went back to her room alone.

So she'd invited him along, going up to her hotel room before him to avoid arousing suspicion. It was a process Louella had quickly learned in Philadelphia.

Now, two hours later, the man was wrestling with his drawers, struggling to put them on. Louella smiled. "I hope you feel better now, Luke," she said slyly.

He looked up at her. "Hmmm? Oh, yeah, of course, Louelly." He missed the leg opening with his right foot again. "I sure do appreciate your kindness to a stranger."

"Need some more help?"

The forty year old man looked at her, then dropped his drawers to the floorboards. "Depends on what kind of help you're talkin' about." He grinned, showing white teeth. "I always did like seconds."

Louella covered her breasts and groin with her hands. "Haven't you had enough?" she asked playfully. "If you get caught with me here—especially by your wife—"

He frowned. "Hell, I don't care what she thinks, or anyone else either." He sat on the bed. "Why don't you come over here and help me out some more?"

Louella jumped onto the bed. They didn't have time to laugh as the mattress bounced onto the floor, already busy as ther flesh melted together and chicken feathers puffed out onto the floor beside them.

Gregory "Shorty" Palmer poured a cup of thick

coffee from the enameled pot and sipped the bitter liquid. He'd just finished his rounds, found nothing, and was taking a well deserved rest in the bunkhouse. His left leg throbbed again, where he'd been shot in a holdup in Denver three years ago. Shorty grinned in satisfaction at how he'd killed the bank guard who'd wounded him, before escaping to safety.

Served him right, the slimy little bastard.

He sure could use the money he'd stolen that day right now, Shorty thought as he looked around the miserable shack. All that gold up in that secret cave—well, not that much gold—and those coins Bucher kept on making—and he was paying practically nothing. He wasn't used to this hard life, working for his daily bread.

Nothing like it used to be, when he'd bought any woman he wanted, drunk whiskey all night and slept all day, spending money like firewood until he ran out. When that happened—which was all too frequent—he'd rob another bank or store, skip town and settle somewhere else where they'd never heard of Shorty Palmer.

The door banged open. "Got any whiskey?" Sam Johnson asked as he walked into the bunkhouse dusting off his hands. "Man, I could use a drink."

"No, drunk it all," Shorty said to the black man.

"Damn! You know how tight Bucher is with that stuff! We won't see another bottle until next month!" The man stared at his friend. "It'd be different if he let us leave this place. I'd ride into town and steal a case of the stuff. Shit, Shorty, you gotta lot of nerve, you know that? You ain't the only man around here who drinks."

"I am this month." Shorty sipped his coffee, grimaced, and threw the cup across the room.

Johnson slid to the left. "Damn! You nearly hit me with that thing!" Johnson said.

"I'm so fuckin' tired of this place!" he yelled. "That damned German and his rules and regulations! It's makin' me fuckin' sick!"

Johnson sat on his bunk across from Shorty. "I know the feelin'. Isn't he ever gonna be done making those damn coins? And when the hell's he gonna let us leave?"

"How should I know? I keep askin' him but he just yells at me to get back to work." Shorty scratched his shirt's stained armpits, sending up an abysmal odor. "And I need a woman. I need one bad."

"C'mon, Shorty, I've seen you with Bucher's squaw, pumpin' away behind the barn." The black man smiled, showing the gap between his front teeth.

Palmer grinned. "Not some Indian. You know what I mean. Some blonde, refined city lady who'll pull up her dress and pull down her bloomers when I tell her to."

"You sure seemed to enjoy old Sour Cunt, tho' Bucher'd cut off your balls if he ever knew."

Shorty rose. "You wouldn't want to go and tell him, would you, Johnson?" He fell onto the bunk and, in a split second, held his knife to the man's neck. "I'd get real mad if you tried something like that."

"Shit no, Palmer. Git the fuck offa my bunk! Jee-suz!"

Palmer flipped his knife closed and stumbled over to his bed. "Just checkin'," he mumbled.

"Man, I'd love to grab those fake twenty dollar coins and get the fuck outa here."

"Tell me sometin' I don't know. You'd never make it. Bucher'd have me kill your black ass."

Johnson sighed. "Hell, you know he wouldn't give you the satisfaction. He'd do it himself."

"Like that damned Indian, Lazy Dick."

"Yeah." Johnson was silent, thinking of their old nemesis. "What if we did it together?"

Shorty shook his head. "Bucher'd track us down and fill us full of lead before we got more'n three miles from this hellhole."

"Then why don't we kill him? Make sure that never happened," Johnson asked intently. "Shit, we could catch him while he's sleeping and slit his throat." The man demonstrated the motion in the air before him.

"Sleep? That old asshole Bucher? Christ, he ain't closed his eyes since we came to work for him. You ever seen him sleeping? I mean *ever*?"

Johnson was silent.

"Hell," Palmer said.

"There's gotta be a way. Think about it, Shorty!"

"There is. We just gotta wait until it comes along." He turned to Johnson. "And Johnson, tell me right now you won't do nothin' stupid like getting yourself so shot up you'll be pissing outa your belly."

The man grunted.

49

Bird Song's tiny moccasins padded the soft
sand trail as she neared the end of her long walk
to the white man's ranch. Her feet ached, so she
sat on a sun warmed rock, enjoying the heat as it
radiated into her body. The eighteen year old
Indian girl slipped off the deerskins and pressed
the soles of her feet against the rock, drawing her
legs up to her chin.

Lazy Eye hadn't returned when he'd left their
camp three weeks ago. She'd waited seven days
without thinking much of his absence, for it was
hard for him to get away without the white man
finding out.

But when her brother hadn't returned by the
time the full moon rose above the pine nut trees,
Bird Song worried. To kill off the uneasy feelings
she'd occupied herself with work.

Every morning she dragged bark baskets of
water up from the lake that had formed behind
the small dam her brother had built in the stream,
then filled the hollowed logs so that the cows
could drink.

She gathered acorns, pine nuts, rose hips,
firewood, herbs to flavor her cooking and heal her
body. Bird Song watered their small, disguised
field of corn on a sunny hilltop, then went about
her camp chores. But after tending the fire,
gathering kindling and wood, mixing pemmican
and leaching acorns before grinding them into
flour for bread, she always felt the aching again.
What had happened to Lazy Eye?

Had the ranch owner been so careful to watch

him that he couldn't sneak away? Was he hurt, or worse?

On rising that morning she knew she couldn't wait any longer. Breathing in the crisp pine-scented air she'd hurried with the heavy baskets, splashing half the water onto the cracked ground as she poured it into the cow's troughs. Bird Song laid freshly cut pine boughs to simulate bushes, disguising their camp, which lay half-hidden beneath a sheer rock mass, then walked quickly toward the ranch where her brother worked.

She'd never been there, but several moons ago Lazy Eye had told her the landmarks he followed, just in case she had to go there sometime. Bird Song memorized them, never thinking she'd ever have to use them.

The Indian girl looked out on the vista before her. Far off in the distance lay Caliente. She'd been to the town several times, but hated the way it looked, smelled and felt. It was ugly and frightening. She far preferred the mission near San Diego where the kindly Spaniard had taught her English ten years before.

Bird Song looked from the town, then to her right at the flat-top tree. Her grandfathers in the sky had struck it with fire from above. It was a blessed, powerful tree, she remembered their tribe's shaman telling her. The leaves could be used to attract a mate if a girl crumbled them in her hands and blew them into his shadow. She gazed at the stunted growth spouting out from beneath the charred, dead wood at its summit.

From this location, Bird Song remembered, she

was almost to the ranch. But she couldn't see it—
not until she'd climbed the hill past the tree.

She slipped her feet back into her moccasins,
brushed the orange dust from her fringed summer
dress, and walked toward the hill.

The sun had crept a half inch lower in the west
by the time Bird Song crouched behind a boulder.
The ranch lay just before her, beyond a fence of
dead logs that stretched out three yards from the
young Indian girl. She jumped over it and walked
up to the largest building she saw.

"What the fuck?" a voice cried out as a man
walked out of the house.

"Please," she said in English.

"Holy shit!" the man said. "What the fuck do
you want, squaw?" a tall, greasy skinned man
asked.

"Lazy Eye," she said.

The man's eyes widened. "Jesus, you speak
English?"

"Yes. Little. *Padre* taught me."

"I ain't seen no Lazy Eye," the man said.

It was hard for Bird Song to understand his
words. "He works here," she said.

In the distance a rider approached the ranch.
"Holy shit, what now?" the man with the accent
asked, turning away from Bird Song.

"Please," she said again. "My brother Lazy
Eye. Where is he?"

"I don't have time for that now, squaw." The
man nervously glanced at her. "I got unexpected
company." Bucher touched his holster
tentatively.

52

The weapon frightened her, but she stood firm. She couldn't leave now. Where was Lazy Eye? "Bucher? Mr. Bucher?" she asked, trying again.

"Yeah. That's my name. Now shut your mouth!"

"My brother, Lazy Eye? He worked for you?"

Horse and rider jumped over the far fence and slowed as they approached the ranchhouse.

Bucher turned to the Indian girl. "Keep your mouth shut until I get rid of this man," he said. "You behave and I'll let you walk out on your own feet. You don't behave—you'll never leave. *Comprende?*"

Bird Song nodded, allowing herself to hope. The man wasn't helping her, but he said he was the one who'd hired Lazy Eye.

She watched as he turned and peered at the rider who dismounted and walked up to them, holding a piece of paper in his hand.

5

"You Emil Bucher?" Spur asked as he walked up to the tall, foreign-looking man standing next to an Indian girl in front of a ramshackle ranch house.

"What's it to ya?" The man eyed him suspiciously, occasionally glancing at the young woman.

The accent was German. Spur knew he'd found the first ranch, according to Weschcke's map. He folded it and stuffed it into his pocket. "Spur McCoy. I'm lookin' for some stray cattle."

Bucher guffawed. "Sure, I'm rollin' in cattle. You can't take a step without landing in cowshit! Fuck, can't you look around you? This ain't exactly the Chicago stockyards," he said sarcastically.

Spur surveyed the scene. The "ranch" consisted of a splintered barn, small timbered house and two outbuildings, one of which must be the bunkhouse, he thought. Six horses were stalled nearby, and four scrawny cattle grazed on the sparse brown grass that had sprouted from the last rains, perhaps six months ago.

"Why're you looking for these cows?" Bucher asked Spur suspiciously.

"Guerra hired me to find them. Seems they wandered off while grazing a couple of weeks ago and still haven't shown up. See ten strange cows around here lately?"

Bucher laughed. "Hell, Guerra's spread's miles away. You won't find them here."

Spur eyed the cattle moving slowly on the upper hill.

"I know what you're thinking, McCoy. Go ahead and check 'em," he said, pointing to the cattle. "They've got my brand all right—a Lazy B."

"Can I take a look around your land?"

The man considered the question, finally shrugging. "Guess so," Bucher said. "But I got to get back to work." He turned to the Indian woman, who stood silently beside him. "We got some talkin' to do," he said, and touched her shoulder.

For five seconds the young woman stared at Spur, as if weighing him in her mind, then wrenched free of Bucher's grasp. She scurried out of his reach and took off at full speed for the trees behind the house.

"Woman problems?" Spur asked, grinning.

Bucher's gaze was cold. "Ain't no woman, she's a squaw. And I don't see how that's any of your business anyway."

"You wouldn't have any other Indians working for you here, would you?"

Bucher looked close at him. "I got a squaw to cook for me. Some law against that?"

"No sir."

"Then leave me the fuck alone. I got work to do." He turned and walked into the house.

Curious, Spur thought. He looked at the trees but the girl had disappeared among them.

For the next hour, Spur rode over the property, half expecting trouble but unchallenged by anyone. He surveyed the surrounding land from the peaks of several hills, but it was as the man said. He saw no cows for miles in every direction. If Bucher had them, he'd either hidden them or driven them to some distant valley. It would take Spur weeks to physically search every valley and hill of the ranch.

He sighed and turned his horse toward the next ranch on his map—one owned by Jack and Peggy Sue Chater.

Three hours later he rode up to a well kept house. The sign over the front gate told him he'd reached Pinehaven, the Chaters' ranch.

A knock on the door produced a redhead who hastily wiped flour off her hands onto her clean apron.

"Can I help you?" she asked pleasantly.

"I hope so, ma'am." Spur tipped his hat to her. "I'm looking for ten cows that wandered away from Don Arturo's place. You seen them around here?"

The woman thought for a moment. "Can't say as I have. But my husband might have. Just a minute. Jim?" she called into the house. "Some stranger wants to know if we've seen any strays."

A sad-eyed, work-eaten man pushed past her and opened the door fully. He bounded out onto the porch. "Are you accusin' me of stealing them?" he asked.

"No, no, slow down, Mr. Chater. Guerra hired me to find those cows for him. I'm just checking the nearby ranches."

"You won't find them here," Chater said. "Christ, it's always the same."

"Jim, your language!" Peggy Sue said, a worried look on her face. "I think you'd better leave. My husband's not feeling too well at the moment. Sorry you had to ride all the way out here for nothing."

"I feel like I'm being—being—blamed for something I didn't do!" Jack Chater said.

"No one's blaming anything on you," Spur said. Chater's reaction puzzled Spur. Did they have the cows? And did he have an Indian working for him?

"Then you can just get your ass off my land," Chater said. "Now!" The man produced an old Army Colt .45. "I don't want to use this on you, but if you don't get off my spread in ten seconds I will!"

Before the man could finish the sentence Spur had blasted a hole through a milk can fifty feet away with his six-gun.

"Sure you wanna use that, Chater?" Spur

asked as his pistol's explosion tapered off.

The man's temper flared. "Just get the fuck out!" he said, and slammed the door behind him as he fled into the house.

Peggy Sue looked at Spur, then frowned. "Look what you've gone and done! And he'd almost forgotten all about it. Sorry, mister, but we haven't seen any cows. Now I think I have to attend to my husband. Sorry we couldn't help you. Good afternoon." She walked into the house.

Spur sighed. His instincts told him that they didn't have the cows. "You wouldn't have an Indian boy working on this ranch would you?" he asked quickly.

Peggy Sue shook her head and slammed the door shut.

An hour later Spur halted his tired horse at a trough outside Arturo Guerra's adobe house. It was huge, spacious, with real stained glass windows. Rows of grapes stretched off for miles to the left of the house, while to the right stood corrals, a cookhouse, what must have been a bunkhouse, and a shack with an anvil in front of it, shaded by an ancient oak. Weschcke was right—Guerra must be fairly successful, Spur thought as he stood on the adobe brick porch and knocked.

After ten minutes of conversation with the man, Spur realized he knew no more about the Indian boy than what he'd told Weschcke. Spur liked Guerra instantly—a big man, with a deep, imposing voice.

"So nothing so far?" Guerra asked him.

"Not yet. I just started on the case this morning," Spur reminded him. "But don't worry, Guerra. I'll catch the counterfeiters."

"What about my two hundred dollars?" the Mexican asked. "Will I ever see it?"

"Don't know, but I hear the cattle weren't worth twenty dollars a head anyway."

Guerra flashed Spur a warning look, then smiled. "Maybe not. But that's not the point. I let myself be cheated! That Indian boy—"

"Got the best of you," Spur said.

"*Si senor—*" He bowed.

High pitched giggling cascaded down the colorfully tiled staircase from the second floor.

"Lupe! Concha! Control yourselves! We have company!" Guerra said. He shook his head. "They refuse every man who comes out here to court them."

Moments later two visions descended the half-circular staircase. Spur held his breath as they walked up to him, afraid they were some part of some daylong dream.

Lupe and Concha were absolutely identical. They wore different clothing, and their hair was done in distinct styles, but they were twins. Incredible!

"Spur McCoy, please meet my daughters Lupe and Concha. That's Lupe on the right."

"*Buenos tardes, Senor McCoy,*" Lupe said, curtseying low.

Concha rolled her eyes at her sister's behavior. "Good afternoon."

"Afternoon, ladies," Spur said, gesturing with

his hat. "I'm glad to meet you—very glad. Marshal Weschcke told me your father had daughters, but not lovely twins."

Lupe rose from her exaggerated bow and smiled. "We don't get many visitors way out here. You from San Diego?" She looked him over.

Spur felt like a cow at an auction house. Not that he minded it. "No," he said. "I'm after some counterfeiters, working with Marshal Weschcke."

"I see," Lupe said. "How interesting." She smiled and ran her tongue over her parted lips.

"*Muchachas,*" Guerra said. "Behave." He turned to Spur. "What can you do with two girls like these?" he asked, throwing his hands up.

Spur could think up a few ideas.

"Arturo!" a voice called from outside.

"Excuse me, McCoy. My foreman calls me. Make yourself at home." He eyed his daughters. "Maybe Lupe and Concha would show you around. Please, my home is your home. I have to supervise some branding for a few hours. We can talk then." He lifted a bushy black eyebrow. "The house will be yours."

"Thanks." Spur watched the man leave. At least he didn't deny his daughters the pleasures of the flesh. "Well, girls, where should we start?"

Lupe took Spur's hand and pulled him toward the stairs. "I have a good idea—what about my bedroom?"

"Lupe?" Concha said warningly.

"All right, your bedroom."

Spur let himself be led toward the stairs. "Are

you sure this is right? I mean, your father—''

"Our father wants us to be happy, so he never minds us having fun. Does he, Concha?''

"Not at all." The girl was more subdued than Lupe, but she walked with them up the stairs and into the bedroom.

Once there they whirled him down onto the plush bed.

"Watch us as we undress," Lupe said.

"Lupe, I don't know—''

"Come on, Concha. You don't want to let a man like Spur pass you by, do you?''

She frowned, studying him, then beamed. "Of course not. If would be a sin.''

"Good." She turned so that Concha could unbutton her dress.

Spur sat on the bed, dazed by the young women's attentions, then settled back to enjoy the show.

"Get out of those clothes, Spur," Concha said in a delightfully accented voice. "We might as well—we've got the time and the feelings.''

Spur did as he was told.

As he pulled off his boots and shucked down his jeans, Lupe dropped her dress to the rug and turned so that Concha could unlace her corset. "Hurry!" she said, pulling down her bloomers.

Lupe's body was an art work—curved where it should be curved, smooth stomach, firm thighs, full, high breasts—everything Spur could possibly want in a woman.

She made no attempt to hide the golden fur patch between her legs as she struggled with the corset. When it finally fell away from her and she'd slid off the chemise, Lupe sighed and walked to the bed, a young boy's fantasy of a woman. She smiled and her breasts bounced as she approached Spur, who sat on the bed, his erection sticking straight up.

"Lupe, what about me?" Concha asked, then giggled as she saw Spur's graphic arousal. "I knew you were a man, Spur, but I didn't know how much of a man!"

Lupe reluctantly hurried Concha out of her clothing, then the two girls, their bodies perfectly matched, unpinned their hair and shook it out.

In unison they approached Spur. He stood and looked at Lupe, then Concha, then Lupe. After a few seconds of drinking in their firm breasts, wide hips and blonde mounds Spur laughed.

"What's so funny?" Lupe asked as she sat beside Spur on the bed.

"Sorry, ladies, but I can't tell you apart."

"Then the only thing you can do is love both of us equally."

"I'm Concha," the standing girl said, as she sat on Spur's left. Her delicate, milk white hand gripped his rock hard penis.

"Me first!" Lupe shrieked. She brushed her sister's hand away and bent at the waist, lips spread wide apart.

Spur's vision blurred as Lupe sucked in the head of his penis. Her mouth was hot, soft, demanding. She continued pushing her head down on his shaft, her throat throbbing and expanding until his pubic hair pressed against her face.

"Where'd you ever learn to do that, Concha?" Spur managed to gasp out.

"*I'm* Concha," the girl to his left said. She lifted his hand and placed it between her legs, then parted them, revealing herself.

Spur's fingers delicately spread her outer lips and tickled her clitoris.

"Oh!" Concha said.

Lupe began working over his erection in earnest, withdrawing to the mushroom head, suctioning it voraciously, then slamming down until he was once again embedded in her throat.

As he continued to finger the other girl, Spur wondered how much longer he could take this.

"Harder!" Concha urged him.

McCoy rubbed and pulled gently at Concha's clitoris, while watching his penis disappear down Lupe's throat.

"Yes! That's it! Rub me raw!"

Lupe turned over, holding Spur in her mouth, until she was on her knees on the bed. He plunged two fingers deep inside her and the woman pulled off him. "I can't wait to feel you inside me!" she groaned.

"My turn!" Concha said, and pushed her sister over on the bed. She opened her mouth and engulfed Spur's already over aroused erection.

His right hand free, Spur forced Concha's head down onto his crotch, reveling in the incredible, liquid velvet of her mouth and throat.

"Damn you!" Lupe said, and knocked her sister's side lightly. "I was enjoying that!"

"You'll make me bite him!" Concha said, wiping her lips delicately.

"Enough of this," Spur said, feeling he was nearly beyond the point of losing all control over the wild twins.

"Let's get to the good stuff!" Lupe said.

Concha nodded in agreement.

The two girls turned and presented their unblemished bottoms to him, then knelt and spread their legs. The perfect, firm cheeks opened, revealing their vaginas. Spur licked his lips.

"Which one of us first?" a voice said.

Faced with a difficult choice, Spur got to his knees and plunged into Lupe first, then Concha, then Lupe again. He rubbed the one he wasn't pumping and both girls sighed as he worked them over. Spur felt his control breaking, so he pulled out and sat back on his heels, panting, sweating, nearly orgasming.

"Stick that cock of yours up my *culo*," Lupe said, wriggling her bottom so that her cheeks bounced gently before him.

"Lupe!" Concha said, turning toward her sister.

"Come on, Spur!" she said, ignoring Concha.

"What does she want?" Spur asked.

"Put it up my ass!" Lupe said, bucking her hips back at him, spreading her hairless, tight hole. "Come on, Spur. I want it. I need it!"

Spur was shocked at the young girl's boldness —but not too shocked. He let his old instincts take over. "Concha, stand over Lupe. Straddle her back.''

Concha turned and looked at him. "Why"

He grinned. "You'll see.''

Concha shrugged and stood on the mattress, then spread her legs and stood over the still kneeling, still wriggling Lupe.

Spur moved close to Lupe then pushed it into her. "Bend over,'' he ordered Concha.

"I—I can't, Spur!'' She started to fall, then placed her hands on her sister's back. "Maybe I can.''

She was open to him.

"I told you I wanted it in my ass, Spur!'' Lupe said, disappointed.

"You'll get it everywhere—just wait, little lady.'' Spur pumped savagely into Lupe, holding her hips, then licked Concha's lips and pushed his tongue up into her. He was surrounded, infused, consumed by womanhood. He inhaled Concha's musky odor as he ate her.

"Oh. Now I understand! Eat me, Spur. Eat me!''

Both girls sighed as Spur worked them over. His hips became a blur as his tongue slapped Concha's button.

They were a three-backed, six-legged sex creature, mutually enjoying each other with total abandon.

"Now. Yes. There! Harder, Spur, oh harder!'' Concha cried. She shook through a climax as she forced her bottom against Spur's face.

He pulled out from Lupe and spat on his hand, rubbed his saliva into his erection, then moved up a few inches. Spur slid the head of his bone hard phallus into the Mexican girl's tighter, higher hole.

"Ahhh," she said, and forced herself back onto him. Spur nearly blacked out as the girl's bottom took his entire length. The heat, the sensations— Spur struggled to take control of his senses.

His testicles bounced against the Mexican girl's cheeks before he slowly withdrew to the head, then plunged back in again. The tight flesh fell away before his intrusion. He started moving in and out of her incredibly tight, steaming hole.

He grabbed Concha's breasts and squeezed them, tweaking her nipples, completely wrapped up in his sexual frenzy.

"Oh God," Spur said, feeling his control beginning to break. The twins shuddered through a second orgasm, then another, as Spur's tongue and organ continued to work them over.

The Secret Agent's cries mixed with those of the girls, and quickly, far too quickly, Spur jammed full-length into Lupe and screamed as he shot his seed deep into her body. His hips jerked spasmodically again and again, each spurt intensifying the sensation tenfold.

As his climax ended he pulled his tongue from Concha's body. Still connected to Lupe, Spur fell on top of her, and Concha on him. The three sweated together, their hearts pounding, racing; their brains fried to prismatic ashes.

Spur shook his head as he gasped, squeezing Lupe tightly with one hand, and lifting his other to grasp Concha's back above him.

Quite a sandwich, he thought, before his thoughts dissolved into a sea of post-sex bliss.

6

"Hurry up, woman!"

Peggy Sue ignored the lock of red hair that brushed against her eyes as she lifted the kettle from the wood burning stove with a damp rag, then hefted the steaming water to the center of her ranchhouse kitchen.

Jack Chater stood before the washtub, his hairy, skinny knees shaking in spite of the warm afternoon air. "If I gotta take a bath you damn might as well hurry! Christ!" He ran his cracked fingernails across his dust-caked chest.

Peggy Sue carefully poured the boiling hot water into the tin basin, then turned to look blankly at her husband.

"Is it hot enough?" he asked whiningly.

"Check it yourself, Jack!" Peggy Sue burst out, then dropped the kettle and hurried out the kitchen door.

"Peggy Sue!" her husband called. "Shit!"

She stopped next to the herb garden and looked down at the purple flowers that had sprouted from the rosemary plant, a treasure her mother back in Virginia had sent with them on their trip west. Her eyes misted. It was happening all over again. She was losing her husband Jack. His language, his anger—and Jack wildly drawing on that nice man that afternoon.

She felt chapped hands touch her shoulders, then a naked man's body press up tightly behind her. "Peggy Sue, I'm sorry," Jack whispered. His hands slipped down her arms and cupped her breasts from both sides.

"Jack," she said.

The man pushed his lengthening organ between her buttocks. "Let's get some lovin'. How about it? Right here in your damn yarb garden!"

Peggy Sue stepped away from him, pulling his hands off her. She turned to look at him. He was half erect.

"Come on."

"Jack, you said that wouldn't happen anymore. You promised me!"

"Said what wouldn't happen?" he asked, nibbling on her ear.

"Going crazy, remembering what happened to you."

"I am crazy," he said. "Crazy about you." Jack Chater gripped himself.

"You know what I mean." The words were harsh. "That was in the past, a long time ago. Can't you let it die?"

Jack sighed and pulled away from her. "What the fuck do you expect, woman? Christ, that man went out and said I'd stolen those cows, just cause I was in jail once. Shit, I never even saw them!"

"He didn't say you stole them."

"He might as well have. I don't know how that damn Mexican found out about me bein' in jail last year," he said, frowning. "It wasn't my fault that preacher was walking by when I was cleanin' my rifle. I was sure I'd unloaded it."

"You were drunk. Let's not go into this again, Jack. I can't take it."

He nodded. "Neither can I."

Peggy Sue's cheeks had colored. She bent and plucked a sprig of rosemary, crushed its dark green leaves in her hand and inhaled the resinous aroma.

"Why not just forget about it, honey, okay?"

She lowered the herb from her nose. "But Jack—"

"Forget it, Peggy Sue, won't you? And I know just how to make you forget."

The woman jumped as her husband touched the front of her dress, then moved to her crotch. "Outside?" she asked incredulously.

"Outside."

What shitty whiskey, Emil Bucher thought as he swallowed another mouthful of the cheap liquor from his flask. He recapped the metal bottle and stuffed it into his mount's saddle bag as he turned the horse toward home.

The sun hung low in the west, nearly obscured by the series of high ridges that seemed to stretch forever. He'd ridden miles over his spread that day, crisscrossing it time and again, and had even moved further out into the surrounding hills, off his land.

He hadn't seen so much as a curly hair of that squaw. And that asshole McCoy wasn't in sight either.

Shit. That was all he needed—trouble. McCoy didn't seem too much of a problem—but he'd be careful. No, it was Lazy Eye's sister that really made his ass itch. Lazy Eye never bothered to tell him that he had a sister, Bucher thought.

Calm down, he told himself. She was just a squaw. No one in town would listen to her, least of all that ass kissing Weschcke, Caliente's "town marshal," whatever the hell that was.

Shit, you got nothin' to worry about. Don't go getting your balls in an uproar. He'd kill the girl if he ever saw her again—no questions asked. Should have gotten her last time but that damn McCoy rode up.

McCoy. Bucher scratched his head. Didn't that name seem familiar? No, guess not.

As he rode home, however, Bucher continued to think about his situation. Now that he'd worked up the fastest possible method of producing the blanks, coating them with gold, and then restriking them in the dies, Johnson and Palmer were making twice as many double-eagles as before. Eight months, he thought. No, six. Six months and he could kiss this hot country goodbye, pay off or kill his men, take the train to San Francisco and look around to find someone who'd be interested in buying the counterfeit coins.

Thirty minutes later Bucher tied his horse's reins at the sagging hitching post before the ranchhouse. "Johnson, where the fuck are you?" he screamed.

"In here, boss," a thin voice called from the outhouse.

"Get the hell out here. Now!"

"Can't a man take a shit in peace?"

Bucher grunted. "I thought you shit out of your mouth, the way you're always lying."

"Christ, Bucher!" The man emerged from the outhouse. "What's the problem?"

"Ride into town. There's a man there—I think. Name's Spur McCoy. He came out here today, snooping around, asking about Guerra's cows or some shit. Find out why he's here."

Johnson's eyes lit up. "You're not sending Palmer, like you usually do?"

"Fuck no, Johnson," Bucher said, smiling. "Hell, he's white and shows up in the dark. You, you don't show up anywhere. Even your blood's darker. Now get the fuck out there and track that man down!"

In spite of the racial slur, Johnson grinned.

"Wipe that thought from your mind, boy! You'll ride out there and then back here. Don't go getting any ideas about not coming back. If you leave you do it with no money. Nothing. If you stay six more months, you'll go with a thousand

73

dollars. Remember that, asshole!"

Johnson nodded and sighed. "Yeah, I remember that."

"Then get your ass moving!"

"Can I kill him?"

Bucher smiled. "Of course, shit for brains! But do it without being seen. And come back!"

"Right, boss," Johnson said, and turned toward his horse.

Spur McCoy stopped to water his horse at a thin stream. He wasn't more than three or four miles from Caliente by now, he thought, and sighed. Nothing to go on. No solid leads.

The Secret Service Agent scratched his stubble covered chin, then ran a hand through his reddish brown mutton chop sideburns, remembering the young Indian girl he'd seen at Emil Bucher's ranch. If he couldn't say anything for the man's manners, at least he had good taste in woman, though the squaw didn't seem to like Bucher much, or at all.

He shook his head and gently reined his mount toward Caliente, planning his next line of attack.

It was just past dusk when Spur rode into Caliente. Soft lights glowed in the windows of the few buildings, and the street was deserted except for a scrawny dog whose padded feet dragged through the inch of dust that had been ground from the hard dirt by horseshoes and wagon wheels.

Spur walked in through the front door of the Buske Hotel as dinner was being served. He ate double helpings of the baked chicken, corn, yams, tortillas and beer. The food was adequate but filling, Spur decided, burping as he pushed from the table. He'd purposely ignored the other diners, still keeping a low profile in town while he worked on the counterfeiting case.

Spur looked across the street at the saloon, and thought of the girls that Weschcke said worked there. He wouldn't have to see them this trip, he thought, as he remembered the afternoon of fun with Lupe and Concha at their father's ranch. That had almost made coming down here worthwhile. Now, if he could only find the counterfeiters.

He walked up the stairs and then down the hall. As he touched the door knob it swung open and the round muzzle of a Spencer repeating rifle jabbed savagely between his brows.

7

Spur stood for a split second as the rifle barrel jabbed against his forehead, then shoved his boot hard into the man's groan. The shadowed assailant howled in pain as Spur sent his forearm flying through the air. It struck the Spencer, sending it whirling to the floor.

"Jee-suz!"

Spur slammed his hotel room's door shut, drove his fist into the man's bobbing chin, and followed up with a jab at the soft stomach for good measure. Two hundred pounds hit the floor and skidded backwards ten feet until the man's head touched the wall beneath the window.

McCoy jumped onto his chest. As Spur reached for his pistol something smashed into his chin, sending him reeling backwards. He nearly lost his balance as his would-be killer scrambled out from between Spur's legs and groped on the floor for the rifle, groaning in pain.

Faint moonlight slanting in through the window showed Spur that the man was black, stocky, scared.

"Talk," Spur said, still groggy. "You've got some explainin' to do." He leveled his .44 at the man's heart.

"Shit, I—"

The door behind Spur opened.

He turned, ready for another assailant, then whirled back around in time to see the black crash through the window.

"Fuck!" Spur ran to the window in time to see the black man roll off the roof, drop to the street, and run like hell around the next corner and out of sight.

"Damn!" No way he could follow him out the window. Spur's head ached and he couldn't think straight. He holstered his weapon.

"I—I must have the wrong room," a feminine voice said behind him.

Spur turned up the flame in the lamp. A young woman with black hair, dressed in city clothing, stood hesitantly in the open door.

"Seems like it," Spur said, shaking his head and cursing himself for letting the man get away. He dusted the floor grit from his hands. "Want to come in and talk about it?" he asked without much enthusiasm.

"Well, I shouldn't." She looked at him frankly. "But why not? At least I know I'll be in good hands—being in your room, I mean." The woman laid a gloved hand against her cheek.

Spur nodded, bent to retrieve the rifle from the floor, switched on the safety and laid it beneath the bed.

"I'm sorry. I thought I'd checked the room number. I'm so embarrassed about getting in the way of your—little tea party." Her eyes sparkled. "Who was he, some jealous husband?"

"No."

"Will he be back?"

"I don't think so, Miss . . ."

"Bucher. Louella Bucher."

The name thundered in Spur's brain. "Did you say Bucher?"

She nodded primly, standing just inside the doorway, seemingly undecided about actually entering the room.

"I need a drink," he said. "You want one too?"

"Sounds wonderful."

He moved to the small table next to the bed and bent to pick up the whiskey bottle that sat there. A sizzling rifle bullet zinged inches above his shoulder, then dug into the wooden wall.

"Down!" Spur shouted to the woman as he slammed up against the wall beneath the window, then peered over the sill.

The shot must have come from a second story building across the street, but Spur had no target. He studied the area for ten seconds, then sighed. "Nothing," he said and cocked his head back toward the woman.

She was struggling with her dress.

"Ma'am—" Spur began, surprised.

Louella Bucher's cheeks were flushed. "I hope

you don't think I'm a fallen woman, but all this excitement has me hotter than a bobcat in August." She finally unfastened the last button and stepped out of the dress. She was completely naked beneath it.

"No, I'm not thinking anything like that at all," Spur said, gulping as the naked woman walked to him.

"I need a man—a *real* man—tonight. Right now! Love me, mister. Love me! I won't take no for an answer!"

She walked unashamedly to him and took his hand.

Wondering if the bump on his head had been more severe than he'd thought, Spur led the woman to the lumpy mattress on the iron frame in the corner of his hotel room.

"Be gentle with me," Louella said, then fell onto her back and spread her legs.

"Gentle? You look like you're ready to be ridden until sunup," Spur said, his groin pounding inside his jeans, straining against the button fly. He rubbed the firm mound as he looked at her.

"This is my first time—with you," Louella said.

The soft kerosene lamp's glow highlighted the dark "V" between her legs. Spur felt his sexual hunger burning suddenly within him. He wasn't about to let the good woman down.

"Hurry up and get naked," she said, squirming over the faded and patched quilts, arching her breasts and sending them wildly bouncing.

"Yes ma'am." Spur stripped quickly, never

moving his gaze from her magnificent body, then sat on the bed beside her. "Do you really want it?"

"Yes!" She said it without hesitation.

"Tell me how much you want it," Spur said savagely, as his arousal throbbed hard against his flat belly, pointing to the sky.

Louella Bucher looked at his crotch and licked her lips. "God, it's beautiful. Don't tease me anymore. Just put it in! Please! Fill me up and make me feel like a woman."

Spur gently squeezed her left breast. "You feel like a woman to me," he pointed out.

"Damnit!" she said.

"All right, all right, Miss Bucher." Spur rose and moved over her, then slowly lowered himself down on top of her.

Louella's body came alive at the contact, writhing in cat-like ecstasy. He crushed her breasts beneath his hairy chest and ground his crotch against hers. Spur slammed his mouth down onto Louella's, then probed in between her spread lips with his tongue, tasting, thrusting it into her throat.

She gasped as he lifted his head, reached down and guided it into her. Louella lifted her legs into the air as Spur's penis touched her velvet opening and slid inside.

A shiver ran through her body. Her back arching, she pressed her hips upward, drinking in every inch Spur had to give her. "Oh God," she said. "God!"

Spur withdrew all the way. "If you don't like it,

say so," he said, taunting her.

"Damnit!" Louella frowned. "I like it. I like it!"

Enough teasing. He rammed back into her, withdrew, then pumped viciously into her tight hole, punctuating each thrust as their bodies slapped together.

"Ahh! That's what I came west for!" Louella said, her eyes shining up at Spur's. "A real man! Ride me, Spur!"

Spur grunted as he slammed into her, then took a breast into his mouth and sucked it. She cooed as his teeth gently scraped across her nipple. She wanted it hard, Spur thought, and he'd give her what she wanted—hard enough so that she'd be spoiled for any man who slept with her after him.

He switched to her other breathtaking breast, mouthing it as if it were the most delicious dessert on earth. It was. He smelled her exotic perfume as he munched and continued driving his erection into her yielding, demanding body.

"You got nice tits," Spur said, lifting his mouth from her.

Louella's body tensed and she threw her head back as she shuddered through an orgasm. Her breasts slowly flushed bright red and she threw her hilt upward. Her mouth formed an "O" and she tightly shut her eyes.

Spur used all the tricks he knew to bring to her another, and yet another climax. He rode her without holding back, reveling in their animal, primal lust. He circled his hips, emphasizing the withdrawal, then the thrust, and rode up high and hard against her clitoris.

"Enough, Spur! Enough!" she said, breathing hard. "I can't take it any longer! Come in me! Shoot it!"

Spur shook his head. "Not yet, little lady. You wanted it, you're gonna get it."

Even as he spoke Spur felt his groin tighten, his scrotum rising closer to his body, preparing for his ultimate pleasure. He couldn't hold back much longer.

"Aw shit," he said seconds later, then his words were lost in a cry of ecstasy as he slammed deeper into her, each thrust faster than the last, until his perfect, masculine rhythm was lost in a welter of lust-crazed, orgasmic emptying, supremely fulfilling moments of complete release.

Spur's body spasmed on top of hers, slick with sweat, as he shot his last and collapsed on top of her. He was crushing Louella but didn't care. Perspiration stuck their bodies together as Louella wrapped his torso in her arms and kissed his cheek, sighing sweetly, then buried her nose in his slick armpit.

They breathed together until their hearts slowed to normal and complete consciousness washed over them. Spur lifted his head and looked down at her.

"Am I too heavy for you?" he asked.

She smiled, satisfied, dreamy-eyed. "No. You're not too anything for me right now."

He smiled and, feeling himself still hard within her, began pumping again.

She jerked in surprise, then rested her heels on

his buttocks and urged him harder, faster, deeper.

"Everything all right in there?" a voice called into the room from the hall. "I heard shots."

The hotel manager, Spur thought, as he drove harder into the yielding woman. "Yeah, fine,' he managed to say, then returned to business.

This time they orgasmed together, and Louella rolled him over until she lay on top of him, their bodies still locked together at the crotch.

After a minute she kissed his nose. "So what else are you good for?" she asked, then laughed.

"Nothing, for a while. You know how to wear out a man," Spur said. He shook his head, laughed, and leaned back against the pillows.

"That's how I like my men—well fucked."

Spur winced at the word. "Miss Bucher, where'd you ever learn to talk like that?" he asked.

"Where else? In bed."

He should have known.

A minute later Spur swung his legs over the side of the bed, wiped the sex mist from his eyes, and reached for the whiskey on the table, then frowned. He stood and pulled on his pants.

"What do you think you're doing?" Louella asked, pouting on the bed.

"Sorry, little lady, but I gotta get rid of some beer."

"Hurry back," she said, and luxuriated on the quilts. "Maybe we can do it some more."

"Insatiable, aren't you, Louella?"

She just smiled.

When Spur returned from the outhouse he

found his room empty. No Louella, no more loving for that night.

Frowning, he downed a swallow of the whiskey and headed for the front desk. "Is there a pretty lady staying here? Looks like she's from the city?"

The thin , balding hotel manager nodded. "Yes. A fine looking piece of woman flesh, I must say." He checked his books. "Here's the entry. Louella Bucher, Room 17."

"Thanks," Spur said, and started toward it.

"It's no good," the thin man said.

"What do you mean?"

The nervous man smiled. "She just walked out the door."

"Did she say where she was going?" Spur asked.

"No." The manager grinned. "But how many places can she go at night in Caliente? I'm sure Miss Bucher'll be back soon, and then you two can get back to it."

Jealous, Spur decided. The man was jealous.

8

Sam Johnson spun around and slammed into the dirt beside the corral on Bucher's ranch. The cold, dry air chilled him.

"You fuckin' shithole!" Bucher blubbered, standing over the downed man, hands on his hips. "I can tell by the look in your eyes that there's been trouble. What happened?"

Johnson coughed, holding his stomach and wincing.

"I knew I should've sent Shorty. Leastwise he wouldn't have dragged his ass back here all beat up, his tail between his legs." Bucher sighed. "What happened, damnit? Did you find McCoy?"

The black nodded. "Yeah, I found him."

"And?" Bucher demanded.

"And . . . nothin'."

"Nothing? Shit!" The German blasted two bullets a foot above Johnson's head. "What happened? Is that bastard McCoy dead? What'd you find out?"

The black man rose to a squat, then painfully lifted himself to his feet. "Hell, man, it was dark. I was lookin' through his room and I heard someone comin' down the hall outside. And then he came in and we fought—"

"And then you killed him." It was not a question.

"Let me tell you how it happened."

"This's like talking to a pile of cowshit," Bucher said and spat on the dirt.

Johnson hid his anger. "So we fought, and then this girl came into the room."

Bucher was interested. "What girl?"

Johnson shook his head. "I don't know. It was dark. So I dove through the window—"

"Chickened out? I should have figured."

"No, I couldn't reach my rifle—"

"He unarmed you!" Bucher said in disbelief.

"Hell, yes, Bucher, he's fast on his feet! So I ran across the street, got my trusty old Army rifle from my horse, tore up these outside stairs, hightailed it across the roof of the saloon, and blasted into his room through the window. He was standin' right there in the window."

Bucher smiled. "So he's dead, right?"

Johnson hesitated.

"Jesus, give me a straight fuckin' answer!"

The man screwed up his face. "I don't know, boss. I heard someone coming so I rolled off the roof and got the hell back here."

Bucher thought for a moment. As the German

scratched his cheek Johnson looked at him with unveiled hatred. Even in moonlight he knew his boss could see the look on his face, but Johnson didn't care. He didn't care about anything.

Soon, he told himself for the thousandth time. Soon you're gonna get your ass away from this place, from Bucher, from the whole goddamned state! Even shoveling horse shit'd be better than having to put up with any more crap from Bucher.

"Since you fucked up this little job, I guess there's nothing I can do about it now." He was silent for a second as he slipped his six-shooter back home. "Maybe you put the fear of God into McCoy and he'll clear out of here. I don't want him snooping around here. Did you find out anything about him? Anyone in town talk to him, notice anything?"

Johnson shook his head. "No sir," he said, shaking his head emphatically. "No one saw him. The manager at the hotel just said he checked in yesterday."

"What about the saloon? He been in there?"

Johnson nodded. "But he didn't talk to anyone."

"And the fancy ladies? Did he get a quick fuck last night?"

"Not so's I could find out." Johnson's gut ached from the impression of McCoy's boot, and he couldn't stand up straight. He also felt a thin trickle of blood oozing from his chin. The torn skin burned.

"Damn! I knew I should have sent Shorty.

Okay, Johnson, that's enough. Get the fuck out of my sight!"

"Yes, boss." Johnson limped to the bunkhouse, tore open the door, slammed it shut and flopped down on the sagging, lumpy, stained mattress. He hurt all over.

As he waited for sleep he heard his employer calling for Shorty. The pains continued until sleep anesthetized his body and brain, and he fell into a world without Emil Buchers.

Gregory "Shorty" Palmer vomited up nearly a bottle of whiskey in the alley outside Caliente's only saloon. The bitter taste in his mouth sickened him, so he spit until his throat was dry, then wiped his bile coated lips and walked back toward the bar.

Before he made it to the bat-wing doors he saw a black haired beauty walking down the street.

Palmer, suddenly sober but feeling like someone had stuck a knife into his stomach and twisted it for a couple hours, knew he needed a woman. Any woman.

He ran up to her and, before she could react, slapped a hand over her mouth, grabbed her waist, lifted her from her feet, then carried her back into the alley. He moved past his puke and leaned her up against the wall. She was curiously unresisting.

He held his face inches from hers. The woman's eyes were wide, wild, but she didn't strain to break free from his grasp.

"Now, I'm gonna take my hand away. Don't scream or it'll be the last thing you'll do. Understand?'' he whispered.

She nodded broadly.

"You know what I want, don't you?''

Again, a furious nod.

"Don't scream.'' He lifted his hand from her mouth.

"The least you could've done was ask me,'' the black-haired woman said as she looked the man up and down. "I usually only let real men fuck me, but I guess you'll do.''

Palmer slapped the woman's face. "Bitch! You think you're hot shit, don't you?''

Her cheek stinging, the woman gasped at him, then grabbed his crotch firmly. She had a strange look on her shadowed face; Shorty couldn't read it, but he automatically pushed against her hand.

"You may be a bitch but you know what to do,'' he said. "Come on. We can have a little fun.''

"Here? In the alley?'' she asked, rubbing her cheek with her other hand as she continued to massage him.

"Sure. Hell, this town rolls up Main Street at sundown and no one goes out after dark. No one but the whores and their customers.''

The woman looked around, then turned back to Shorty. "Well,'' she said. "You've got a pretty nice one—and it sure does get hard.''

"It'll fill you up right nice,'' Shorty said. His erection pressed painfully against his fly. "Let me take it out and show it to you,'' he suggested.

The woman shook her head. "I don't think so.''

Shorty's temper flared. "You don't think so? Just what're you gonna do about it?''

"This!'' She punched his crotch with a small,

tight fist, sending shockwaves of pain radiating through Shorty's body.

"Goddamn bitch!" he screamed, doubling over in agony.

Before Shorty could cover his bruised genitals with his hands the woman sent her knee firmly into his groin, then lifted her skirts and fled down the alley toward the hotel.

"Fuckin' shit," Shorty said, and rolled to the ground in a fetal position, rubbing his bruised balls and rapidly shrinking penis. "I'll get you, bitch!" he vowed, then blacked out as his testicles sent up another round of pain through his central nervous system.

"Goddamn it, Shorty, where the fuck are you?" Bucher yelled, then shook his head and stormed into the barn. Probably sleepin' off a drunk, he thought. He lit a lantern with a sulphur match. As the flame brightened and grew he searched the barn with the light. Shorty wasn't there.

That bastard wouldn't have ridden into town, Bucher thought. He blew out the flame, hung the lantern on the nail next to the doors, and checked the hitching post. Shorty's mare was gone.

"Shit!"

Bucher knew he'd been too lax with the man, letting him ride into town once in a while for some fun with the ladies. Now the bastard must think he could just ride out whenever he felt like it. Damn!

Bucher thought of Johnson as he headed for the ranchhouse. Suddenly he was having problems with both the black and Shorty. Only since that bastard McCoy showed up. The German knew he should have sent Shorty into town to find out what Spur was doing there, but if nothing else, the man would be dead by now and no further possible trouble from him.

He sighed. Time to get some new men. He'd have Shorty blast the worthless Johnson into bits, hire the next likely man he could find, then kill Shorty and replace him with another hand.

Just can't get good help these days, Bucher thought, as he tipped a bottle of rotten whiskey up to his lips and let the burning liquid pour into his mouth.

"No, Weschcke, I didn't get a good look at the man," Spur McCoy said minutes after Louella Bucher had vanished from his hotel room. Caliente's town marshal had heard the shot, finally saw McCoy's broken window and hurried into the hotel. "But he was black, stocky— that's about it."

"Black? That's strange. Not many around here. More in San Diego. Ever see him before?"

Spur shook his head. "Not as far as I know."

Weschcke sat on the warped chair in Spur's room and frowned, running a finger through his full, white beard. "I'll ask around. Heard about a black working on a ranch, but don't know which one."

"You remember where you heard it?" Spur asked.

Weschcke shrugged. "In the saloon. Some yahoo talking about all the things he hated about Caliente. That was one of them," she said frowning.

Spur took it in. "He could be connected with the counterfeiters," McCoy said.

"But no one knows you're in town checking on that, do they?" the marshal asked.

"Not as far as I know. I haven't exactly been spreading around the news," Spur said with a sarcastic smile.

"As long as you're in one piece I can rest easy. When I saw the broken window and found out it was your room I expected the worst." He rose.

"I can take care of myself."

"I can see that. You've had one hell of a night. Get some shuteye."

"I'll try, Weschcke."

"And I'll ask around tomorrow morning, see if anyone saw a black man in town tonight."

"Thanks," Spur said, trying not to think about the sleepless night ahead of him, six-shooter in hand, eyes darting from his hotel room door to the window.

Louella Bucher slipped into her room, flustered, out of breath, but smiling. She'd sure shown that man, hadn't she? Not that she would have turned him down, if he'd been nice to her and hadn't smelled like vomit. She shuddered, reliving the experience, then began undressing for bed.

Spur McCoy, she thought, and smiled. The way he'd rolled her she wouldn't need another man for a month.

Or a week.

A day?

Louella smiled and unpinned her hair. She wasn't at all sorry she'd passed up the brute.

9

The next morning, after breakfasting in silence in the hotel's kitchen, Spur walked to Weschcke's office, rubbing the small bump on his head, a souvenir from his encounter the previous night.

He found Wallace Weschcke snoring at his desk. The town marshal's feet were propped up, and his hat pulled low over his eyes.

"Morning, Sheriff," Spur said loudly after banging the door shut. He walked into the man's office.

Weschcke lifted his hat, placed it farther back on his head, and slowly rose up in his chair, yawning. "Morning, McCoy." He rubbed his eyes.

"You look like hell," Spur observed. "Been there all night?" He took a chair.

"Yep. Figured I better, just 'n case Caliente had anymore excitement, or if you needed me. At least I got caught up on the gossip last night.

Everyone stopped by who was up late and jawed over coffee. I heard Emil Bucher's daughter arrived in town recently—she's staying at the hotel. You meet her yet?"

Spur nodded. So the pretty woman was Bucher's daughter. He relished the thought of the man knowing what he'd done to her in bed. "Got to know her pretty well. But hell, Weschcke, you could've gone home. If I'd needed you I would have gone there."

The man shook his head. "No good. You'd never wake me up by knocking. And I usually keep the place locked up—I've sent my share of men behind bars, here and in other small towns. Hell, when there's an emergency—and there's damn few of those, let me tell you—the local men just fire off a couple rounds outside my place. That always wakes me up. Besides," he said, sighing, "I'm used to sleeping in this here chair."

"What about your deputy?" McCoy asked. "Can't he stay here at night and let you get your rest?"

The lawman laughed shortly. "Don't have one, much as I'd like to. Hell, this is a small town— Caliente's not big enough to support two lawmen."

Spur nodded. "Understand. In all the excitement last night I didn't remember to ask you some questions about the ranchers I met yesterday."

"That's right," the big man said. "It was yesterday you rode out there. What'd you find?"

"Not damn near enough," Spur said, grinning.

"But I need your opinion on the people."

Weschcke eyed the empty coffee pot that sat on the cold stove. "Shoot."

Spur smiled at the comment. "Talked to the Chaters, Jack and Peggy Sue. What kind of folks are they?"

"The Chaters—well, they're a nice couple," Weschcke said. "Moved here from back east about a year ago. Bought the old Regula ranch and are working it well, from all reports. Peggy Sue and Jack are good, clean-cut young kids."

"Really? Surprises me to hear you say that. Jack Chater went crazy while I was there. He pulled a six-shooter on me and threatened to use it if I didn't get off his land. I managed to talk him out of it with some fancy shooting of my own."

Weschcke's yawn ended quickly. "Jack Chater said he'd kill you?"

Spur nodded. "Sure seemed anxious to get rid of me."

"Hmmm. Can't quite believe Chater'd do a dumbass thing like that," the man said wonderingly. "Shit, that boy hasn't given me a day of trouble all the time he's been out here." He looked at Spur, his eyes bright. "What'd you do to set him off?"

"Nothing. I was just asking his wife about Guerra's missing ten cows—that's my excuse for being out here; I say Guerra hired me to find them. When I mentioned the cows Chater lost control." He paused. "Maybe he has something to hide."

Weschcke smiled and waved off the notion. "Hell, I bet I know what made Jack Chater fly off the handle." The man ran his fingers through his full, snow-white beard. "This is just gossip and hearsay, you understand."

Spur nodded.

"Okay. Jack Chater spent twelve months in jail back East somewhere. Unnerstand, McCoy, those kids are tighter'n clams about this. Touchy, you might put it."

"Why'd Chater get locked up? Counter-feiting?"

"No. Seems old Jack was three-quarters of the way through a bottle of good whiskey when he decided to go outside his house to clean his rifle. He 'accidentally' killed a preacher who happned to be walking by—he was so drunk he forgot to unload it. The judge sentenced him to a year in jail. The Chaters left town right after he was released and moved here."

Spur thought hard for a minute. "A man can learn a lot of things in jail."

"Maybe. But anyway, Chater could've thought you knew about his past and assumed he'd stolen the cows, especially if he'd been drinkin', which it sounds like he was. Like I said, he doesn't like to talk about it."

"Is this Chater the criminal type?" Spur asked.

Weschcke chuckled. "Not at all. Drinks too much, but then we all do. He's a fine, upstanding man. A little ornery, maybe, but he isn't a counterfeiter, if that's where you're getting to."

"We don't know that for sure," Spur said. "Can't rule him out. I didn't see any cows with

Guerra's brand out there, though, and when I asked if they had any Indians working for them—thinking they may have sent one of their hands to buy Guerra's cattle—Mrs. Chater shook her head."

Weschcke rose to his feet, went to the pot-bellied stove that stood in the center of his small office, and began fueling its firebox from the pile of sticks and twigs that lay between its feet. "Gotta get some gut-rot brewing," he said. "It's the only thing that really wakes me up."

"Chater sure did act strange," McCoy observed. "And he's been in trouble with the law before."

Weschcke broke a small branch over his knee, then stuffed it into the stove. "Shit, I don't know, McCoy. Maybe you've found the right track. He hasn't been out of jail long. Chater's working hard to start a new life, earn some self-respect. He just might be desperate enough to take a short-cut. A man in Chater's situation might do anything." He paused, frowning. "Maybe you're right—he's a possibility."

He'd talked himself out on the subject. "Before I hit Chater's ranch I stopped by Emil Bucher's spread."

Weschcke looked up and laughed. "You mean 'Bucher's Folly'?" he asked lightly.

"Yeah, I guess so. I talked with the man for a minute or so. Is that what his ranch's called in town?"

"Yep," Weschcke said. "Should be obvious why, since you've seen it. That 'ranch' doesn't earn him a goddamned cent. He's living on practically nothing and keeps to himself. Folks around town call him 'crazy.' I just think he's a Pennsylvanian who didn't have enough brains to buy good land when he hauled himself out here.''

Spur was silent, thinking.

"I don't suppose you saw Guerra's cows out there, did you?" Weschcke wiped his hands on his knees, then bent to light the fire.

"No. Rode around for a few hours. Didn't see any cattle but a few skinny ones on a hill just above his spread. If he had them Bucher could've hidden them, but I doubt it."

"Seems pretty harmless to me," Weschcke said, his voice booming resonantly in the office. "I'm thinkin' Bucher'll stay on here until his money runs out, then run back East and give Caliente one less joke to throw around while we sit in Laurel's saloon tipping back beers."

He carefully lit the bone dry wood, then closed the squat stove's door and resumed his seat behind his desk. "Bucher doesn't come into town too often—once a month for supplies, or to get a quick one at Laurel's. To tell you the truth, I really don't know much about him—except that he's a damned bad rancher."

"Bucher had an Indian woman with him," Spur said. "Actually she couldn't have been more than eighteen or nineteen. They didn't seem to get along too well."

Weschcke snorted. "Hell, everyone knows Bucher's a squaw man. Maybe that's why he doesn't come into town too often, and when he does it's usually after dark."

Spur nodded. "Maybe."

"You make it out to Guerra's place too?"

"Yes. Talked with him and met his daughters—Lupe and Concha. Quite a pair."

"Yeah," Weschcke said, his eyes alive. "Two pairs, from what I can remember. Nice, firm, young pairs!" He smiled, obviously relishing the picture in his mind.

"That too." Spur smiled, recalling their afternoon together fondly. He'd rarely met a woman—let alone two—who loved sex as much as they did. He shook off the memories. "But Guerra couldn't tell me anything more than what he'd already told you."

"I figured as much," Weschcke said. "What's your next move?"

"Don't know. Maybe try to talk to the Indians—I didn't get out to the reservations yesterday. No time."

"You know where I am if you need me, McCoy," the town marshal said.

Spur nodded and left the office. It was a good question, he thought. What *was* his next move?

Bird Song rose from her bed of ferns and sweet sagebrush leaves at dawn, thew back the deerskin hides that had locked out the night's chill, then glanced at the place beside her, as she did every morning.

No. Lazy Eye hadn't returned in the night.

She felt her throat constrict again, and for the first time the young Indian girl contemplated a life without her brother.

Somehow she'd avoided the thought, clinging to the belief that one day Lazy Eye would run into camp as usual, breathless, excited. He'd tell her his latest adventures and help her with work.

But every dawn as she awoke alone her hope was killed off a bit more. Now she had none left.

Downcast, Bird Song straightened the skins and knelt beside the ash covered coals. Patiently she blew out the lower coals with long, sustained breaths until a tiny yellow flame emerged from them. Bird Song set a handful of crumbled oak moss onto it and the fire blazed up, waking from its nighttime sleep.

After building a small cone of branches over the rapidly growing fire she took a drink from the bark basket, rubbed some of the cool water onto her face, and sighed.

A breakfast of pemmican, wild berries and acorn bread didn't satisfy her as it usually did. With Lazy Eye—even though he'd spent only one or two nights out of fourteen—she'd felt comfortable, secure. The eighteen year old enjoyed living in the old ways of her people.

Bird Song's father had been killed the day after she'd been born. When her mother had died ten years later Lazy Eye had taken her to the Spanish Mission on a hill overlooking the marshy San Diego bay, where she worked hard, learning new things, trying to block out the senseless pain.

A few years later, when she was ready to go on with her real life, she'd made the two day journey on foot with Lazy Eye from San Diego to the hills lying near where Caliente eventually was born, toward the sun but far from her beloved blue ocean. They'd searched for days to find the perfect site to make a permanent, year-round camp. Near water, pine trees and oaks, sheltered from the wind spirits, easily hidden in case of trouble.

Now, Bird Song thought, she had no father, no mother—and no brother. Her tribe had either been massacred by the roundeyes or scattered hundreds of miles away. The Indian girl was without a people. She was totally alone.

Bird Song fought the tears that threatened to roll down her high cheekbones as she set three blackened, heat resistant rocks onto the fire, positioning them so they'd absorb the heat. She had work to do, the Indian girl told herself. It was time to make black sage tea, for the nights were growing colder and her throat hurt all the time.

As she waited for them to warm, Bird Song sank back onto the soft dirt, gazing at the rising sun. Life without Lazy Eye, she told herself, wouldn't be life at all.

She could go back to the mission, where Padre Francisco had seemed genuinely friendly to her.

During her stay at the mission they'd spent many long nights arguing over her ways of contacting the unseen. Everytime she'd mentioned the spirits in the plants, the sky, and the stones, or spoke of her ancestors' whispers in her ears, the Padre had thundered to her about Satan's deceptions.

It was more than she could take.

Bird Song sat in contemplation for ten minutes while the rocks warmed, then filled a tightly woven basket with fresh water from behind the dam Lazy Eye had built in the creek. She delicately transferred each rock into the water, holding them with a piece of pliable bark. The liquid hissed on touching the rocks. A minute later it was nearly boiling.

Bird Song crumpled a handful of the dark, strong smelling black sage leaves she'd gathered a week ago and sprinkled them onto the water, wondering again what she would do if Lazy Eye never returned to their camp.

A cow's lowing in the distance reminded her of her new responsibilities. The ten creatures were dumb, slow things, but she'd grown to love them in the past three weeks because Lazy Eye had brought them to her. He'd arrived in camp unusually excited, saying they'd make them rich. After carefully explaining how to care for them during the time he was away he'd left and never come back.

They're probably thirsty, Bird Song thought, and automatically rose to fill their drinking troughs, trying to block out her fears of the future.

Emil Bucher pushed the middle-aged Indian woman off his bed. She landed on the floor and laughed raucously.

"Good-for-nothing bitch!" Bucher said. "Cook me some eggs. Make yourself useful or you'll be out on your butt before you can wipe your pussy!" he thundered.

The woman rose, smirked, and flounced from the room, her plain black cotton skirt accentuating her hip's swing.

Damned heathen squaw isn't worried, Bucher thought, disappointed, as he hurried into his clothing. She knows no other woman—white, Indian or Mexican—would come close to his ranch. She was far from the best fuck he'd ever had, but was close by and could cook pretty damn well too. All he gave her was a closet to sleep in, some of the food she prepared, and daily rations of his male seed.

Lazy Eye's sister sure was better looking, he decided, slapping a weak brimmed, dirty hat onto his head as he headed for the kitchen. He remembered the curves of her youthful body beneath her primitive leather dress. If she ever showed up there again he'd throw her on her back before killing her. She'd be a nice change of pace from his old squaw and the fussy whores in Caliente.

Bucher walked into the kitchen, smelling eggs sizzling in fat on the stove. "Hurry up!" he yelled. "I'm hungry!"

The squaw lifted her skirt and showed him her bare bottom.

"For food, damnit!" he yelled, and dropped into a chair.

After watering the cattle and checking to see that they had plenty of grass to eat, Bird Song disguised her camp and began the long journey to the outskirts of Caliente. She hid behind a Jeffrey pine tree, pushing her nose against the rough bark and smelling the rich, sweet scent as she tried to summon the courage to enter the town. A few men walked down the dusty street, and a brightly dressed blonde woman strolled on the broken boardwalk.

You have to go in there, Bird Song told herself firmly. She had to talk to someone about Lazy Eye—maybe he'd been seen in town.

A hundred yards from her, doors exploded open and a man staggered out into the street, holding a bottle of what Padre Francisco had called "the Devil's mix." He dropped it and fell onto the ground.

Bird Song turned away. She couldn't talk to them, couldn't face another white man after what had happened at Bucher's ranch yesterday.

Still tired from her walk, the Indian girl turned and headed toward her camp, fearing that she'd never again have the courage to walk into the white man's town and ask about her brother.

She was fearless—certainly no animal frightened her, from the largest snake to the huge, hairy legged spiders that lived in the hills. Nature was a part of her life.

But she feared what she might find out about her brother. Bird Song put extra effort into her steps as she slowly made her way up through countless dry valleys and gulleys toward her camp.

Tomorrow, she told herself. Tomorrow she'd make herself ask the white men where her brother was.

10

Louella Bucher paused before her hotel room door and stared at the number—17. She was sure it was 17. How she'd ever walked up the stairs and went into room 27 yesterday still surprised her. Not that she'd minded, meeting that nice man with the huge hang—what was his name? But she was afraid she'd given his opponent the advantage in their little scuffle.

Well, nothing she could do about it now, Louella thought, as she entered her room. She threw back the curtains and luxuriated in the full sunshine streaming in through the window.

The young woman was torn with conflicting emotions and thoughts. She knew she should arrange to hire a carriage and ride out to her father's ranch, but she didn't even know where the place was, and besides, once she was out there —if everything went well with him—her life of

107

pleasing herself with men was over.

She was enjoying Caliente—no prissy ladies running around discussing the latest hats from New York, no men in three piece suits with gold watch chains barging past her on the way to the street cars. They were decent, honest people here —and the men, thought Louella. The men!

She'd certainly found out what they thought of her father. As she sat to eat breakfast that morning, she couldn't believe the chaos that nearly ensued once she mentioned her name.

"Louella Bucher!" one man said, and laughed. "Mercy. You kin of Emil Bucher?"

"Yes. I'm his daughter. Anything wrong with that?" Louella asked, curious. What was he laughing about.

"Not as far as I can see," the cowboy said lewdly, grinning at her.

It wasn't until the huge bowl of scrambled eggs was passed around that she asked the man what he found so funny. Her cheeks burned as she stated her question.

"Oh, you know; everyone around Caliente knows. It's kind of famous—Bucher's Folly."

"Well, I'm not from around here, and no, I don't know."

The man smiled. "Your father's ranch," he said, and shoved a forkful of potatoes O'Brien into his mouth.

Louella sat down her tin coffee cup. "What about it?" she demanded politely.

He laughed again, infuriating her. Louella turned to the four others present at the table.

"Can anyone here tell me what this *gentleman* is talking about?"

An elderly, white-haired woman dressed in fancy-lady clothes nodded. "Oh yes, child, but you might not want to hear it. You seem like a nice young woman, and I hate to bear bad news. But your father's ranch is well, kind of a joke around this town."

Her mouth hung open. "A *joke*?"

"Yeah, Laurel's right. He's a crazy man," the bald man said. "Living out there, raising rocks on his ranch. He'll never amount to anything. Emil Bucher's probably the worst rancher in the great state of California."

Louella pushed her plate away. "I don't believe it!" she said. "I don't believe any of this!"

"Suit yourself," the man said, and returned to his eating.

"Why would we lie, dear?" Laurel said.

She looked at the white-haired woman. "I don't understand," she said, frowning. "In his last letter my father wrote me that things were going well."

"Not from what I hear," the elderly woman said, shaking her head. "Seems Emil Bucher just wasn't the kind of man for ranch work. Does he know you're coming to see him?" she asked hesitantly.

Louella shook her head.

"Oh dear. Well, no use worrying your pretty head about that now. Eat up, girl. You're as skinny as a spring lamb. You gotta have more meat on your bones to please a man!"

Louella found she'd lost her appetite. She pushed her plate away.

"I hope things go well for you when you see him," Laurel said to her as the woman pushed around the sausage on her plate.

"Thank you." Louella's voice was uncertain.

"Sorry you had to hear it like this, but it's probably all for the best. At least you've been warned. Best of luck, girl," the woman said, and shook her head gently.

Louella rose from the table and left the hotel's kitchen, then walked to her room, pouting. They had to be wrong. They *had* to be!

Her father couldn't have changed that much. Crazy! Not working? She remembered him as he was before her mother had been killed by that bullet during the morning train holdup. He'd been warm, loving, hard-working, a perfect father.

Then he'd quickly started to change after that —his wife's premature, senseless death had embittered him. He began drinking heavily, never went to church anymore, and seemed to lose interest in everything, including his daughter. So he sent her to live with his sister, Agnes, in Philadelphia.

When he'd left for California Louella hoped he'd come back happy and ready to get on with his life, but now she wondered if that would ever happen.

She sighed again and sat on her bed. She'd go to his ranch tomorrow morning—she couldn't possibly face him today. She hadn't seen him in six years, and wanted to look and feel her best before confronting him.

Besides, Louella thought, if she didn't go until tomorrow, she might be able to see that man again tonight and get some more lovin'.

What was his name?

Shorty Palmer looked through the cracks in the bunkhouse wall. Emil Bucher wasn't in sight. He knew Bucher'd sent Johnson out to the mine a half mile away to crack out more of the free gold. This should be a good time.

Shortly slipped out from the bunkhouse and nonchalantly walked to the barn, went inside, and closed the door behind him.

The saddlebags lay on a rickety table next to the stove. Sunlight streaming in through a gap in the roof timbers revealed the glint of gold.

Bucher had just finished coating the base metal blanks with the yellow ore, gold, restruck them in the dies to get the perfect impression, and slipped them into the saddlebag while Shorty made up five more of the blanks. Then Bucher had told him to take a nap while he went in and threw a quick one into his squaw.

Shorty approached the saddlebags, his scuffed boots moving quietly on the straw covered, packed dirt floor. There they were, within reach. Bucher'd never miss five double-eagles, would he? No. He didn't think so.'

The short man killed off the desire to take the whole saddlebag, mount up and ride like hell out of the place. Bucher wouldn't miss five of the coins, probably, and he wanted to wait his employer out to see if the man was serious about paying him a thousand dollars when they were finished with the counterfeiting operation. That would make all his hard work—and all the bullshit from Bucher—worthwhile.

Not that he trusted the man. Ne never knew if his employer would blast two holes through his heart some night as he slept in the cold bunkhouse, but he was willing to wait and take his chances. Besides, he slept light.

But he needed whiskey—more whiskey than Bucher gave him. And he could keep Johnson in line if he gave the man some too. Plus, his tangle with that bitch in town the other night gave him a taste for women, though it had certainly hurt his pride, and the fancy ladies of Caliente charged double what they did in San Diego—four dollars for a fuck, five if he wanted them to lick him all over—and he meant all over!

So he needed the fake coins. He'd buy some whiskey and a white woman, and then get the hell out of town. Shorty'd avoid going back there until he absolutely had to.

He thought of Lazy Eye for a moment, just before reaching into the bag. The same thing wouldn't happen to him as had happened to the dead Indian, he thought, and pushed five of the coins into his pocket.

As he did so the barn door opened.

Shorty whirled around, swinging his .44 up from his holster, and blasted two slugs toward a moving target before he'd really sighted it.

Bucher's squaw, screaming, eyes widened with fright and pain, dropped to the ground, her hand covering an inch-wide hole in her chest. She cried out once in an unintelligible language, then closed her eyes. Her last breath rattled out of her and she lay still.

Shit! That damn squaw! Bucher'd kill him for this. Thinking quickly, Shorty dragged the woman's body next to the saddlebags, stuffed the five double-eagles from his pocket into her hand, and then stood next to the door waiting for the inevitable.

"Jesus Christ, what the fuck's happening here?" Bucher thundered as he ran into the barn. He nearly tripped over the dead woman. "Shorty, explain this!" he demanded.

"Yer squaw has sticky fingers. Caught her tryin' to steal the coins," Palmer said, holstering his weapon. "I didn't think about it; I just shot her."

Bucher stared hard at Shorty, looked at the woman, then back at his hired hand. "This true? You ain't bullshittin' me, are you, Shorty?"

"Hell no! You always tole me to kill whoever got too close to the damn coins. I did it automatic, like." Palmer struggled to keep his fear from his voice.

"Shit," Bucher said. "Never pays to get involved with bitches."

He was fooling him, Palmer thought. He was fooling him! Good. "I'm sorry, boss," Palmer said, shifting his weight from foot to foot as he stood uneasily next to his employer.

"Couldn't be helped. Hell, she was a lousy cook anyway. I guess I'll have to get my lovin' in town from now on." He shot a glance to Palmer. "You

113

too, eh, Palmer?''

Shorty started to protest, but Bucher laughed.

"Don't worry, I ain't gonna cut your balls off, though I wanted to when I saw you with her one morning. But hell, I figured you must've been fucking her for some time. A hard dick's got no conscience. I didn't mind as long as you didn't wear her out.''

"But boss—''

He grinned. "And I figured it was better, your humping her. If I didn't let you get away with it, I thought you might start on the horses, or mebbe try fucking Johnson's fat black ass some cold, lonely night.'' He grinned lasciviously at him, pumping his hips in the air.

Shorty laughed nervously. "Shit, boss, I'd never push my cock into—''

Bucher waved off the man's comments. "I don't give a shit what you think you'd never do. What the hell, a hole's a hole. I'm partial to pussy, but if it ain't around I'm not proud.'' He laughed. "Shit. Woman troubles! Whenever you meet a bitch you know there's trouble ahead. Nothin' you can do about it now, Palmer. You did right.'' He frowned at the man.

"Thanks, boss,'' Shorty said uncertainly.

"Dig another grave and cover her up before she starts to smell.'' Bucher walked to the woman, took the five double-eagles from her hand, laid them on the table and spilled out the saddlebag's contents beside them. He quickly counted the coins, then turned back to Palmer. "What're you waiting for, Palmer?''

"Nothin'." He walked slowly from the barn.

Got out of that one by the skin of your teeth, Palmer thought, and smiled as he once again got the rusty shovel. He'd have to find another time to steal a few double-eagles, but figured Bucher'd probably transfer them to the safe in the ranch house quicker than he had that day. He'd bide his time.

That morning Spur knocked on Louella Bucher's door again, half expecting her not to answer.

"Who's there?"

"Spur McCoy," he answered.

"Who?" She paused a moment, then pulled the door open. When she saw his face she smiled. "Oh! I thought I recognized that deep voice," Louella said, excited. "Come on in, man after my own heart!"

Spur tipped his hat to her and stepped past the woman.

"Where'd you run off to last night, after you'd tired me out? Thought we were gonna have seconds."

"I ran straight to the nearest church to pray to God to remove my sinful desires," she said with lowered eyes, her hands pressed together before her.

"I don't believe you," Spur said. "Besides, there's no church in Caliente."

Louella laughed musically and raised her shoulders. "Okay. I went walking in the night air, thinking about what I'm going to do here. Have a seat, Spur."

"Thanks." He dropped into the chair by the window. "What are your plans?"

"Well, I'm here to see my father," she started hesitantly.

"Emil Bucher?" Spur guessed.

She looked at him. "Yes. Do you know him? Seems like everyone around here does," Louella said sadly.

McCoy shook his head and threw his hat onto the bed. "Don't know him, but I met him. Had to ride out to his ranch yesterday on business."

Louella sighed and sat beside his hat on the bed. She picked it up and fingered the felt. "Folks here in Caliente seem to regard my father as the local joke."

"That's what I heard," Spur said gently. "Does he knew you're going to see him?"

Louella shook her head. "No. I know I should have sent a telegram from Philadelphia telling him I was on my way, but I didn't have time, and they don't have a telegram office here anyway. So I just packed my bags, walked out of my aunt's house, and took the first train west." She paused. "Every day I'm thinking more and more that maybe it was a mistake."

"Why?"

She smiled. "I don't know. I don't seem to know much of anything anymore. This place has me confused."

Me too, Spur thought. He was no closer to finding the counterfeiter than he'd been before he arrived. "What kind of man is your father?"

Louella put her hands behind her and arched

her back, highlighting her perfect breasts. "Before my mother was killed he was kind, warm, loving. After that he started to change. Now—I don't know."

Spur figured the young woman had some surprises in store for her. He kept remembering that Indian girl he'd seen on Bucher's ranch. Louella might not like the father she'd find here in Caliente.

"How are you getting out there? It's quite a way," Spur asked gently.

"I was thinking about renting a carriage tomorrow morning, but I'm not sure I could find the ranch—even if I got a map showing me the way."

Spur nodded. "I've been there. Want me to escort you? I'd be glad to go along."

Louella glowed as she sat upright on the side of the bed. "Would you? That would make it much easier for me. I'm not used to these wide open spaces—and I keep hearing about the Indians around here."

Spur laughed. "They're nothing to worry about. Most of them were slaughtered as soon as the Spaniards and Anglos started moving in here."

Her eyes misted. "How terrible! This was their home. They were here first!"

"Yeah, that's the way I feel too, Louella, but that's the way of this world. No one ever said it was fair. What time tomorrow morning do you want to leave?"

"I don't know. Maybe right after breakfast?" She looked at him, studying his face.

"Sounds fine. Can you ride a horse, or should I

hire a carriage?"

"If I was going by myself, a carriage. But seeing as how you'll be along with me a horse is fine. I'm used to riding—my aunt and I rode every weekend at her summer house in the country outside Philadelphia."

"Great." Spur stood.

"Where do you think you're going?" Louella asked, pouting. "You can't leave yet, you just got here! And besides, I thought we could continue where we left off last night."

"I really should—" Spur began.

Louella rose, bent over him, and quickly pressed her slick lips against his.

Spur moaned during the kiss.

"You really should what?" she whispered, lifting her lips and nibbling on his ear.

"I—I don't remember."

"Good."

What the hell, Spur thought, as he reached for the woman. Nothing he could do today anyway. He hadn't gotten any sleep last night, watching for the sudden reappearance of the black man, and didn't relish the idea of an all day ride to the nearest reservation. Might as well get some more pleasure in, since this beautiful young woman was practically on her knees begging him for it.

Besides, he'd have a good excuse to look over Emil Bucher's ranch again, maybe find out a few more things, when he escorted her out there tomorrow. Who knows, Spur thought, the man wasn't any good at ranching. Maybe he was good at counterfeiting coins.

11

Spur and Louella spent the afternoon loving until dusk fell. They had dinner in the hotel and then Spur went off to inform Marshal Weschcke that he was escorting Louella Bucher to her father's ranch tomorrow, and that he'd take another look around the place. Then he flopped down onto his mattress for a well deserved night of rest.

Hours later, Spur woke to hear his room's doorknob turning.

He sprang up, instantly alert, and grabbed his holster from the headboard.

The door opened and a woman's silhouette appeared in the hall.

"Spur?" Louella asked softly.

He smiled, laid down the holster, and rose. "Come in, Louella."

She walked into the shadowed room. "Where are you?"

McCoy walked up to her and touched her shoulder. "Here. You back for more, little lady?"

"No, not necessarily," she said, turning to him. "Unless you want to. I really just didn't want to sleep alone tonight. I'm worried about my father, and what I'll find when we go out there tomorrow." Her face, gleaming in the moonlight, was tense. "Could I sleep with you tonight, Spur?"

He smiled. "Of course."

"Great!" She undressed then, laying each article of clothing carefully on the chair, then slipped naked into bed next to Spur.

He pressed his body against hers from behind, wrapped his hairy arms around her smooth ones, and they slept platonically until morning.

Deborah, the youngest girl working the saloon in Caliente, caught the eye of a short man who'd been drinking for two hours at the bar. She walked up to him and smiled broadly.

"You want some lovin'?" she asked.

"Sure." He slammed the bottle onto the bar, put his arm around her shoulders, and walked upstairs with the young girl.

Once in her room she undressed quickly, pulling off her dress, then her camisole, garter belt, and stockings. She laid naked on the bed.

Her body was young, nearly perfect. The breasts were smallish, with huge unaroused nipples.

Shorty, already aroused, jumped onto her, spread her legs and jammed inside. He rode her so roughly the girl's head banged against the wall each time he drove into her.

"Not so hard, cowboy!" she said. "You're splitting me in two!"

"Shut up!" Shorty yelled. "I'm paying for it, and I'm gettin' my money's worth. So stop complainin'."

Fifteen minutes later, Shorty was buttoning up his shirt.

"Four dollars," Deborah said, still nude on the bed.

The man grunted and flipped a double-eagle onto the mattress.

Deborah's eyes widened as she saw the coin. "I don't have any change, mister," she began.

"Keep it, You deserve it."

Deborah moved to the floor, knelt, and crawled up to Shorty. She licked their combined juices from his limp penis just before he stuffed it into his pants. "Thank you, mister! I'll be able to retire early!"

He smiled and walked out the room, down to the saloon where he bought two bottles of whiskey with his last double-eagle, then rode towards the ranch before Bucher found him missing from the bunkhouse.

He'd taken a big chance, stealing the two coins only hours after he'd killed the squaw that morning, and then leaving that night, but figured that if Bucher found any missing coins he'd just blame it on her. She could've been stealing for weeks or months.

Five minutes after her customer left Deborah walked down the hallway to Laurel's office. She proudly handed the double-eagle to her madam.

"Twenty dollars?" the white-haired woman exclaimed, then laughed raucously. "Hell, what'd you have to do for that, lick his asshole?"

"Nope. He just likes me, I guess."

"I guess so." Laurel flipped the coin in her hand. Her smile faded. "Wait a minute, Deborah." The vivacious, elderly woman sat at her cherry wood desk, laid the coin on it, and scratched its face with her fingernail. "I'll be damned!" she exclaimed. "Deborah, that man fucked us both!"

"What?"

"Counterfeit. It's a goddamned counterfeit coin!"

Deborah whistled. "I've been screwed!"

Bird Song watered the cattle as usual, then hurried to disguise the camp with fresh pine boughs. This morning she was going to go into town and ask about Lazy Eye. She had to!

The journey didn't seem so long this time, and Bird Song enjoyed watching the hawks circling high overhead as she walked along the barely perceptible trail.

This morning she'd dreamed. Her grandfathers had sent her a vision. Lazy Eye, wearing a new loincloth, walked out of a huge cave holding a white bird.

She called to him, but he didn't seem to hear her. The walls of the cave glowed like sunlight and were hung with countless red pine cones. Each seemed to be on fire, yet the cones themselves weren't consumed by the flames, didn't turn to ash and drop onto the ground.

Lazy Eye looked up, smiling, and let the bird fly from his hands. It flapped for a moment above his head, then flew to the cave wall and took one of the pine cones in its beak. It instantly turned bright red and, aflame, rose from the cave and flew straight up into the clouds.

Suddenly Lazy Eye shrank. He was a ten year old boy, crying at the cactus thorn stuck into his foot. Then he fell to the ground on his back and melted into a baby, crying soundlessly while he kicked his stubby arms and legs.

The baby disappeared and Bird Song had sat up, fully awake after her vision. Her stomach growled as she looked up at the sun just rising above the far eastern ridges.

What had the vision meant, she wondered as she neared the town? What had her grandfathers been trying to tell her?

Was he alive?

She shrugged off the question, knowing the spirits would help her understand when the time was right.

Bird Song put new vigor into her steps. What the vision hadn't told her, maybe the white men could.

Guillermo, one of Arturo Guerra's ranchhands, rode up to the adobe house, hastily tied up his mount, and tore off to find his boss, one hand on his head to keep his sombrero from flying off. "Don Arturo!" he yelled.

"What?" Guerra asked, looking up from where he squatted beside a dying grape vine.

"I found the cattle!" he said in Spanish.

The Mexican stood. "Where?"

The man was out of breath. "In a box canyon miles from here. No one was around, but they were penned up, and had been given grass and water. Someone was taking care of them."

Guerra nodded. "Good work, Guillermo." He slapped the man's shoulder. "Drive them back here soon as you can."

"Yes, Don Arturo."

As Guillermo rode off Arturo dusted his hands on his pants legs. At least he wasn't out the ten cows, the man thought, staring at the dying grape plants. But he wasn't satisfied. He still wanted the Indian who'd cheated him, not for the sake of justice but to kill off the guilt gnawing away at his guts. He'd allowed himself to be cheated—unforgiveable.

He'd tolerate a lot, and had in his life, but not that. Not that!

"Get your ass out of bed, Shorty," Bucher yelled as he walked into the bunkhouse. He kicked the mattress as the man continued to snore away.

Palmer yawned and wiped sleep grit from his eyes. "What is it, boss?" he asked, as Johnson stumbled to his feet on the other side of the building.

124

"I've been thinking this morning. Might as well take care of a problem before it gets you by the balls. That damned Spur McCoy—he saw Johnson the other night. Aren't many blacks working around here, and he might just be smart enough to figure out who sent him into town."

"So?" Palmer said, sitting up in bed.

"So get your ass into town and kill that fuckin' McCoy! Track him all day if you have to, then plug him when you can do it without being seen." He turned and looked at Johnson, who stood stretching his arms in his stained, dirty shorts. "And do a better job than Johnson."

"So how do I find him?" Shorty asked, slapping down a piss hard-on as he rose and stood beside his bed.

"He's in room 27, the Buske Hotel," Johnson said quickly.

"Right. And McCoy's a big man, about six feet, two hundred pounds. Reddish brown hair, muttonchop side burns. You'll see him. Not many men in town anyway."

"Okay, boss."

"And don't fuck up! All I need's more trouble around here." He shot a glance to Johnson.

"Shit, what'd I do?" the black man asked.

"Nothin'. That's why I have to send Shorty into town to finish your goddamned job!"

"But you never tole me to kill him!" Johnson protested. "That was my idea!"

"I don't give a shit! You don't leave something like that half-finished." He looked at Johnson critically, then shrugged. "Turn around and face the wall," he said to the man.

"What?"

"I said turn around and face the wall!" Bucher thundered.

As the man did so Palmer watched the proceedings with increasing interest.

Bucher looked hard at the man, but Johnson's shorts covered what he needed to see. He walked to him and roughly yanked them down, revealing fat, hairless buttocks.

They'd do, Bucher thought, if he ever got desperate enough. As long as he didn't think about what he was doing it might even feel like he was fucking a black woman's ass. The German was surprised to feel blood rushing to his groin. Might as well try him out right now.

"Boss, I don't understand!" Johnson protested.

Bucher drew his .44 and waved it in the air as the man turned toward him. "Don't give me any trouble and I won't kill you. Lie face down on your bunk." He glanced at Shorty, who grinning, crossed his arms on his chest.

Johnson's eyes widened. "Shit, you're not gonna—"

"Do it!" He aimed at the man's naked crotch. "My dick or a bullet. Which one you want?"

Johnson looked around desperately for a second. "Shit!" he said, and walked to his bunk, kicking off his shorts.

Bucher laid his gun down, lowered his pants to

his ankles and approached the black man, who lay trembling.

"Boss, I—"

"Shut up!"

Palmer sat on his bunk, slowly stroking himself, as he watched his employer kneel on the mattress between Johnson's splayed legs.

Fifteen minutes later Bucher rose and hastily pulled up his jeans, panting. Johnson lay motionless on his bunk.

"Hell, Shorty, you enjoyed watching that, didn't you, you fuckin' pervert?"

"It was different," the man said, wiping his seed from his stomach with an old sock.

"Now that you've had your little fun, get your ass to town and kill Spur McCoy, or I'll fuck your butt next time!"

Palmer looked at Bucher as he pulled up his pants. "If you ever try that I'll—"

"Don't give me that shit," Bucher said, cutting off the man's words. "On second thought, if you don't kill him don't bother showing up here. Ever again! That clear in your fuckin' pea-sized brain?"

"Yeah, clear enough," Palmer mumbled.

"Good!" Bucher stormed out of the bunkhouse.

Shorty Palmer stared at Johnson, who lay sniffling on his bunk, as he dressed. "You okay?" he asked.

"Shit—I guess so. That fuckin' bastard! I'd

never let him do that if he didn't have that gun!''

"I know,'' Shorty said. ''You don't have nothin'
to explain. I'm just lucky it wasn't me.''

"I'll kill the bastard next time I see him!''
Johnson kept his face to the wall. He couldn't
look at Shorty.

"Right,'' Palmer said. ''But if you don't you
might as well get used to it.''

"Get fucked!'' Johnson said savagely to the
wall.

Palmer smiled and pulled on a flannel shirt,
then pushed his hat onto his head.

"You rode into town last night, didn't you?''

"Yeah.''

"Thought I heard you leavin'. What'd you do?
Fuck one of the whores?''

"Yeah. It was great.''

Johnson was silent a minute. ''What'd happen
if I told Bucher what you did?'' He looked over
his shoulder at the man.

Shorty frowned, then grabbed his crotch.
'You'd get this before I slit your throat,'' he said,
and laughed.

"Shit,'' Johnson said, and sighed. ''How'd I
ever get up here?''

"Same way I did.'' Shorty strapped on his
holster and walked to the door. ''Bad luck.''

"What the fuck am I gonna do?'' Johnson said,
wincing as he sat on the bed.

"Bend over and spread 'em whenever Bucher
walks by,'' Palmer suggested with a grin, then
walked out.

12

Wallace Weschcke hurried to his front door, grumbling as he sloshed hot coffee onto the floor. As he opened it a well dressed old woman entered.

"Come on in, Laurel," he said as the woman barged past him.

"Sorry to take you away from your breakfast, Wally, but I've got trouble." She paced, clutching her beaded purse to her side with gloved hands, lips tight.

"What kind of trouble? Some man trying to get it for free?"

"Worse than that—if you can imagine." She fumbled in her purse for a minute, then produced the counterfeit double-eagle and held it out to Weschcke.

"You're paying me? I thought men pay you—or your girls," he said, laughing.

"This isn't funny," Laurel snapped, then

pushed a strand of grey hair into the bun at the back of her head. "Turn it over."

He did and whistled. "Counterfeit," he said.

"Some boy passed that to Deborah last night. I knew it was fake the minute she gave it to me." She snapped her purse shut and threw it onto the settee.

Weschcke shook his head and put the coin down. "I didn't think you had any Indians come into your establishment," he said, and drunk a sip of the hot coffee.

"Weren't no Indian—it was a white man. He sure got his money's worth—worked poor old Deborah over right good. And then he gave her this!" She threw her hands up in the air. "What are you gonna do about it?"

"I'll keep it, if you don't mind. Add it to the other ones I have." He set down his coffee cup.

She sniffed. "I heard about that. Old Guerra got some a few weeks back, didn't he?"

Weschcke nodded. "From an Indian."

"This wasn't no Indian. I remembered seeing him go up with Deborah, after she'd described him to me."

"What's he look like?"

"Oh, short—real short. About 5' 5", maybe 5'6". Skinny as a rail—he looks underfed. Dirty clothes. Haven't seen him in town much, and he's only been to my place a few times in the past year." She frowned. "And Deborah tells me he ain't much below the waist, not that that'd help you. Had the dick of a twelve year old boy."

"You'd recognize him if you saw him again?"

"You bet I would!" she said savagely. "Imagine him, thinking my girls do it for free! And poor Deborah, out her honest dollar." She shook her head. "What's happening around here? Is everybody turning crooked?"

The marshal smiled. "Some folks would think what you're doing ain't exactly legal."

"Hell," she snorted. "Ain't no laws against men and women having a good time. Leastwise, not in Caliente."

"You know I don't bother you, Laurel." He sighed. "Anything else you can tell me about him? What color's his hair?"

"I don't know. He wore a hat. All the men wear their hats—even while they're with my girls."

"I suppose he won't be back in town for quite a while. He's gotta know people would get wise to him sooner or later."

"Thank God it was sooner. I talked to Peter, behind the bar. He checked his cash box and found another counterfeit twenty dollar coin like that one, but he wouldn't give it to me. Told me he'd bring it in himself. Said he got it from the same sonofabitch." She grimaced. "It gets me to wondering how many other people he cheated in town."

Weschcke nodded. "I'll check with Max at the general store and at the stables. You keep an eye out and if you see him again come get me—it doesn't matter what time, day or night. Okay?"

The spry woman softened her hard expression somewhat. "Okay, Wally."

He kissed her pale, lined cheek. "And maybe

I'll be able to come visit you again real soon."

Her face broke into a smile. "That would be quite nice. Any time you want, you just stop by. On the house." She winked.

"Thanks, Laurel," he said, and watched her leave.

Louella met Spur outside the Buske Hotel, dressed in a plain cotton riding dress, her hair pinned up under a bonnet that was securely fastened beneath her chin. He'd tied two saddlebags with a few of her belongings onto his mount.

"Ready to go?" he asked, as he stood beside the horses.

"As ready as I'll ever be." She frowned. "I'm not sure I want to go out there."

"Let's not go through that again. You have to sometime," Spur reminded her. "Might as well be today."

"You're right, of course. I'm just being silly. I came all this way and I'm not turning back now," the young woman said firmly.

"Good girl."

Spur helped her into the saddle, then mounted beside her and the pair rode slowly out of town.

McCoy was impressed by Louella's riding skills; she controlled the strange animal beautifully, holding the reins with a steady, assured hand and toeing the horse's flanks firmly but gently.

"Where'd you learn to ride like that?" he asked

her as they rounded a small rise past the huge, broken orange boulders that dotted the countryside.

"Back in Philadelphia. My Aunt Agnes had horses stabled at a friend's house and we'd go riding every Saturday afternoon. Sometimes we went on fox hunts," she said, sighing. "I hated the hunt and she knew it, but she kept on taking me, hoping I'd fall in love with one of the rich old men that always attended."

"How come no man's taken your hand yet? You're beautiful, intelligent, and don't whine. That's three qualities I admire in a woman."

She smiled at the compliment. "No man may have taken my hand, but lots of them have taken everything else."

"Louella, the way you talk!"

"I don't know, Spur. I guess I'm not ready for marriage. At twenty-five I'm not sure I'll ever be ready."

"It's never too late,' he said softly as they rode together, smelling the sweet scent of sun-baked sagebrush and chaparrel.

"Now you're sounding like my father used to talk." Her face fell. "I can imagine what he'll say when I see him—'Where's your husband?' I'm not looking forward to facing him."

He slowed his horse to her mount's exact pace and reached over to take her free hand. "I'll be there, at least part of the time. If things don't work out you can come back to town and stay with me."

"Thanks for letting me stash my things in your

room, Spur. I'm glad you didn't talk me out of it. Guess I shouldn't take anything for granted from here on in."

"Probably the best thing you could do. Your father—"

She turned to him, withdrawing her hand. "Yes? What about my father?"

Spur hesitated. He thought of the Indian girl. No sense in telling Louella her father was a squaw man.

"Well, what about my father?" she demanded softly.

"Nothing. You know the years out here have changed him, like they do all men. You might not like what you see."

She sat up straighter in the saddle. "I'll just have to see," she said, and kicked her mount to a slow gallop.

An hour later they approached the front gate of Bucher's ranch. Spur dismounted, opened the weathered wood, then walked his horse onto the property beside Louella.

"I—I can't go through with this," she said and reined her horse to a halt.

"Louella, do it," Spur demanded. "You know you have to."

She sighed. "Okay."

As they neared the hitching post beside the small house Louella's expression grew grim. "It doesn't look like a working ranch—not that I know what one would look like. Where's the cattle? The horses? The money?"

Before Spur could answer Bucher bounded out from the house.

"Shit, I thought I recognized you," he said, staring at Spur. Then he stopped and glanced at the woman on horseback. A second later his expression changed. Color flooded his cheeks and he wiped the dirty hair back from his eyes. "Louella? Is that you?"

"Father!" she said, jumping from her saddle and running to him.

The German gathered her up in his arms uncertainly, then laid his cheek on her shoulder. "Louella. What in blazes are you doing here?"

"I—I—" She smiled, breaking off the hug. "I wanted to see you," she said.

"Well, I'll be a—" Bucher started, then fell silent. "It's been a long time. My, you've grown up into a fine young woman." He lifted her pale left hand and studied it. "Not married yet?"

She blushed. "Why, daddy dear, you don't think I'd do such a thing without asking you first, do you?"

Bucher smiled. "No, guess you wouldn't." He looked at McCoy. "Say, wait a minute, don't tell me you're marrying him!"

Louella laughed. "No, father. Mr. McCoy was kind enough to escort me out here. I didn't feel safe riding out here all alone."

Relief washed over the stocky German. "Good. I mean, all right."

"Mr. Bucher," Spur said in greeting.

"Mr. McCoy." He reluctantly looked at his daughter. "I can't get over how you've grown. How's your Aunt Agnes?"

"Well, when I saw her last. I—I didn't tell her I was coming out here."

"You didn't? Why in hell—I mean, why not?"

"I didn't want to worry her, so I left and sent a telegram on the way." She looked at him seriously. "Are you happy to see me?"

He put his hands on his hips. "I'm—yes, hell yes I'm happy to see my baby girl! Why shouldn't I be? I'm just surprised, that's all." He managed a thin smile. "You should have told me you were coming."

"I didn't have time. One morning I just packed a few traveling bags and went to the station."

"Well, I'm glad to see you," Bucher said, putting on his best face. He turned to Spur. "Thanks for escorting my Louella out here safely, McCoy. She's fine now. You can leave."

Spur approached the pair. "Is that all right with you, Miss Bucher?"

She frowned. "No, it's not all right! Father, can't we at least offer the man some coffee?"

"Don't have any brewing,' Bucher said darkly. "And I'm not set up for company," he said to Louella. "Sorry, McCoy."

"That's okay," Spur said. "Should be heading back anyway. Good seeing you again, Bucher. And it was nice meeting you this morning, Miss Bucher."

"Nice meeting you too," she said, turning back to him and winking.

He started tying up Louella's horse.

"Don't bother," the man said. "I can do that. Just go about your business."

Spur nodded, stepped into the stirrup and rose to the saddle. He tipped his hat. "Miss Bucher," he said, and rode off.

Five minutes later Spur halted his horse in a small stand of live oaks on a hill overlooking Bucher's ranch. Louella and her father must have gone inside, for no one was in sight.

He waited an hour, watching the place, and saw no one. Finally, just as he was about to leave, a man walked into the barn. From that distance McCoy couldn't tell if he was white, black, or Indian.

Bucher's ranch was a hot bed of activity, Spur thought wryly as he went to his horse. He figured Louella was safe for the time being—her father seemed somewhat pleased to see her, mostly surprised, but disturbed at the same time.

He sighed as he rode down the hill toward Caliente. Though he feared for Louella's safety, he realized it wasn't any of his business. He had to find the counterfeiters.

Bird Song wandered aimlessly among the boulders and infrequent trees near Bucher's ranch. There, she knew, she could find out what had happened to Lazy Eye. But she didn't have the strength or the courage to face the angry white man again. She knew that if he ever saw her again he'd kill her.

He'd made that plain the last time, when the handsome horseman had ridden up and broken off their short conversation. Her instincts told her to run and so she had, away from possible danger but also toward continuing doubt and despair.

The young Indian girl sat on a rock and, for the first time in weeks, cried.

As Spur's horse was picking its way slowly down the rocky hillside a rifle shot echoed through the area, bouncing off mountains and thundering past him at 284 miles per second.

Must've come from Bucher's ranch, McCoy thought, and savagely spurred his horse. The beast whinneyed and galloped down the hill, avoiding the larger rocks with agile steps.

He hoped Louella was still in one piece by the time he got there.

13

Three minutes after hearing rifle shots Spur rode
in through the opened gates onto Bucher's ranch.
He slowed his cooperating mount as he neared
the hitching post. No one in sight. He hastily tied
the mare's reins.

"Bucher!" he yelled.

The man appeared in seconds in the ranchhouse's doorway. "You back again, McCoy?
What do you want?"

"I was riding by and heard a rifle. Thought
there might be trouble."

"No," a voice said from behind Spur. "Had to
kill a lame horse."

"Strawberry broke a leg?" Bucher asked the
man, red-faced.

"Yeah. Fell into a hole on my way out. Nothing
else I could do," a short man said.

"Shorty, you did right." Bucher motioned to

the man. "Guess you won't be doing much riding until we can replace Strawberry. Get back to work."

"Yeah, boss," the man said, eyeing Spur curiously. "Shouldn't I—"

"Just get your ass back to work!" Bucher said between his teeth.

"Right." He backed away, then turned fully and disappeared into the barn.

"Anything else I can do for you?" the German asked Spur.

Louella opened a window and waved at the Secret Service Agent.

Seeing her, Spur relaxed immediately. "No, don't think so."

"Then I suggest you leave."

Spur nodded and unhitched his mare. "Just checking," he said.

Bucher walked toward him. "I don't see why I have to keep on explaining myself to you. I appreciate your bringing Louella out here safely but leave us the fuck alone!"

"You're welcome." Spur blew out his breath as he mounted up. Maybe he'd acted too hastily, expecting the worst, but he wasn't sorry he checked up on Bucher. Not that McCoy expected the man to kill his own daughter an hour after seeing her for the first time in six years.

He didn't envy Louella, living with a man like Bucher on that doomed, damned ranch—Bucher's Folly.

While he was riding back to Caliente McCoy surveyed the land on either side of him. It was primitive, almost primeval. He couldn't imagine the awesome forces that had thrown the huge rock masses, now weathered into smooth, gigantic pebbles, out onto the land.

As he was passing a particularly large rock formation Spur saw an Indian girl sitting in its shade. She was staring at a spiderweb that caught the late morning's sun.

He halted his horse as she turned to look at him, frightened.

"Don't run away," he said gently. "I'm a friend."

The girl stood, poised, ready to move, then sank back onto the ground.

Spur recognized her—she was the one he'd seen on Bucher's ranch. He knew she was skitterish, so he slowly dismounted and stuffed his hands into his pockets to show his peaceful intentions.

He stopped twenty feet from her. "Anything I can do to help?" he asked in a hesitant voice. "Do you speak English? *Espanol?*"

She nodded, eyes lowered.

"Which one?"

"English," she said.

That's something, Spur thought, chalking up a victory. He'd made her talk. "Are you having problems?" He walked a few feet closer, slowly.

She nodded and leaned against the shaded rock.

"Problems with Emil Bucher?"

She looked at him in fright and then bobbed her head again.

"Want to talk?"

Bird Song was silent, still.

This wasn't getting him anywhere. "Were you Bucher's woman?"

The woman cocked her head curiously. *"Que?"* she asked.

She does know some Spanish, McCoy thought. "Bucher's woman? Did you live in his camp?"

Her eyes brightened as she understood. "No." The girl vigorously shook her head. "Never." She shivered in spite of the intensifying heat. "I *pitshe* him. Hate him."

"Then what's the problem? Why were you there the other day?"

She studied him, tight-lipped, the way she'd done when he'd first ridden out to Bucher's ranch.

"Trust me. Friend," Spur said.

"My brother," she finally said.

"What about him?" Spur advanced two more paces, six feet.

"Gone. Almost a whole moon now. Every day I want him to come back into camp. He does not." She dropped her head.

Gently, Spur told himself. "Why—"

"My brother, he worked for Bucher. We made a camp four miles from here. He lived at the *rancho* and came to see me when he could. Then, he did not come. Now I look for him."

"His name?"

"Lazy Eye." She turned to Spur, approaching cautiously. "You have heard of my brother?" she asked eagerly.

Spur shook his head. "I'm sorry, but no." Almost a moon ago, Spur thought. Over three weeks. That's about when the Indain passed the bogus twenty dollar gold pieces to Guerra. Could there be a connection between Lazy Eye, Bucher's ranch, and the counterfeit coins?

"And you went to Bucher's *rancho* looking for Lazy Eye?"

She nodded. "Yes. But I have no help there."

I can imagine, Spur thought wryly. "What did Lazy Eye do for Bucher?"

She rubbed her small hands together. "I know not. He did not talk about it."

A possibility. The Indian couldn't have made the coins himself, not without equipment, a smelter, and stolen dies. Maybe his employer made them, Spur thought.

"Please. Help me find Lazy Eye!" she pleaded.

Spur smiled and nodded. "I'll do what I can," he said. "But it's a big country."

She tilted her head again.

Spur paused. "Lots of places to look."

The girl frowned. "I know. I look. I find him not."

"What's your name?" Spur asked.

"Bird Song." She looked up into a nearby pine.

"And your people?"

"Gone. We were *Ixtonche*, The People."

"I'm sorry," Spur said.

She smiled half-heartedly. "I want my brother. If you hear of him, come to my camp."

"Where is it?"

Bird Song looked at him guardedly.

"I won't tell anyone. Where can I find you?"

She pointed. "From that mountain, straight ahead to a hill with old metates, where we ground acorns, south of the stream." She sighed. "Come if you find out."

Spur nodded as she turned to go and was instantly swallowed up behind the giant rock.

He didn't see her again as he rode away toward Caliente.

"Fuckin' shit-for-brains! What the hell are you doin' back here?"

Bucher and Shorty Palmer stood on the far side of the barn moments after Spur had left the second time. The German lowered his voice so that his daughter wouldn't hear them.

"You were supposed to kill Spur, and then he rides in here—with my daughter!"

Shorty's neck grew red. "Hell, what'd you think I should do, walk all the way out there? Weren't my fault Strawberry got her shoe caught in a hole a mile out!"

"Enough excuses! Borrow one of the other horses, hightail it to Caliente and plow that bastard into the dirt! And you better do it this time, or it's your ass! You know what I mean!"

Anger constricted Palmer's throat. "Yeah."

"Then I'll make you die slow, you bastard! Get out of my sight before I kill you right here!"

Palmer slammed his hole-ridden hat onto the dirt, stomped on it, picked it up, shoved it onto his head, and stormed off.

Bucher breathed hard for a minute, then with an effort calmed himself as he turned to more pressing problems—his daughter.

Louella couldn't have picked a worse time to visit him—goddamn that insolent daughter! She couldn't wait six months until he was through with the coins. They'd be nearly impossible to hide from her—unless he could figure out a way of getting her to leave the ranch.

Bucher scratched his belly as he walked to the house. Problems, problems. Shit! He'd never get rich this way.

Furious, Shorty picked Bucher's fastest, healthiest horse and raced off the ranch, then slowed down when he thought of what he had to do. Normally, he'd jump at the chance to go into town with the old man's blessing. Now he worried.

You're a fool, Shorty told himself. Spending those fake coins in town last night. If anyone figured out they were counterfeit, remembered who spent them, and saw him on the street, there'd be hell to pay.

He couldn't walk the streets in Caliente safely. Not for a long, long time. How could he kill Spur without being seen?

Palmer let the horse have its way at a slow walk, ambling off the slight path in the general direction of Caliente, thinking.

After stopping to piss, Palmer had just buttoned up his fly when he saw a young Indian girl walking toward him. His male instincts took over.

Shorty ran for her. The girl shrieked as he easily overtook her and wrestled her to the ground.

"No!" she said.

Palmer slapped her, hard, then ripped off her leather dress. Her young, soft body lay naked on the light brown dirt, the sunlight revealing every detail.

His mouth watered at the huge areolas, pointed breasts, smooth, flat stomach and her nearly hairless mound.

"Hot damn!" Palmer said, holding down her wrists over her head as he pressed his legs onto hers.

"Please!" she cried, shutting her eyes and gyrating below him.

"Please? Hell, you don't have to ask me for it." A quick rip at his crotch with his right hand opened his fly. His erecting penis dropped out onto her bare stomach.

At the sight of the man's arousal Bird Song went limp beneath him.

"That's better," Shorty said. "I like a woman to fight it, but it's easier if she don't." Still holding her arms, Shorty stroked himself to full hardness, then spread her legs with his and lowered himself into position.

"No," Bird Song said helplessly.

"Young one, ain't ya? Yeah, bet you're a virgin too. Nothing like cherry pussy."

He pushed savagely, missing her vagina and sliding up onto her belly. "Fuck!" Shorty cursed. Guiding his phallus he forced his way between her tight, dry lips, then savagely ripped apart her hymen and plunged deep into her mysteries.

He was going to enjoy this, Shorty thought, trying not to remember what he had to do in town that day to a man called Spur McCoy.

14

Marshal Weschcke wasn't in his office, so Spur
checked the saloon and found the man draining a
glass of whiskey. He sat beside the lawman and
ordered a drink.

"McCoy!" Wescheke said. "Good to see you
again."

"You too," Spur said.

"Any news?" the town marshal asked.

"Let's not talk here."

"Fine with me."

Spur downed his drink, paid for it, and the two
left for Weschcke's office.

"I can't be too careful," McCoy said as he
paced in Weschcke's office a few minutes later.
"Never know who might be listening in on your
conversation."

"I agree. Oh, Guerra rode into town this
morning with good news—seems one of his men

found his ten good-for-nothin' head of cattle penned up in a box canyon out in the hills. Someone must have been watching them—their troughs were full, and fresh grass was laid in for them to eat. They're back with him safely."

Spur grunted. "So at least he's not out anything. Any idea who penned them up there?"

The marshal shook his head and ran a finger through his full white beard. "No. His man didn't find anyone near the critters. But when he went out to bring them back he passed what looked like an Indian camp nearby. No one there."

"Was it near a creek, beneath a huge cliff?" Spur asked.

The marshal looked up, surprised. "Yes. You know something you're not telling me?"

Spur shrugged. "I escorted Emil Bucher's daughter out to her father's ranch this morning. On the way back I met an Indian girl. She told me where her camp was, in case I wanted to talk to her again."

"What about this Indian girl?"

"She said her name was Bird Song from some tribe I can't pronounce. She'd been looking for her brother and asked my help. Said his name was Lazy Eye. Ring any bells?"

Weschcke frowned while thinking. "No, can't say it does. Indians come and go around Caliente, but we don't have any town Indians. None of them ever seem to stay that long."

"This Lazy Eye used to work on Bucher's ranch. But about three weeks ago he left the camp he shared with his sister and never returned."

Spur paused. "That's just about when Guerra sold his cows for those bogus gold coins."

"Yes," the town marshal said slowly.

"So this Lazy Eye might have been the one who passed the coins to Guerra."

"Possibly."

"Something could have happened to him after he bought the cows—could've been killed by someone else who found out what he was doing. I doubt he made them himself. Lazy Eye—or whichever Indian it was—must've been paid with them, or stolen them."

"Hmmmmm."

"If this is true, it doesn't put Emil Bucher in the best possible light."

"No, I see your point." The man scratched his head. "You think Bucher's the counterfeiter?"

"Maybe. Or maybe not. Just because this Indian worked for him, and an Indian passed the double-eagles, doesn't mean horseshit. I need proof."

Weschcke shook his head. "Sorry, Spur, but I just don't think Bucher's the type. He's crazy, but not that crazy. Besides, something else happened last night—two more counterfeit coins showed up in town."

Spur stared hard at the man. "Where?"

"In Laurel's place. You know, the white-haired woman who takes her meals at the hotel?"

McCoy nodded, remembering the woman. She didn't try to hide the fact that she ran the fancy-lady house in Caliente.

"Deborah, a cute little girl, got one from a

customer, and the bartender was paid another one for a couple of bottles of whiskey."

"Do you have a description of the man?" Spur asked, thinking.

"No. Neither Deborah or Laurel were much help. Except that he was short—5' 6" or so."

Spur smiled. "I saw a man about that height out on Bucher's ranch."

"So you're bound and determined to prove he's responsible for all this, McCoy?"

"No, it's my job to find the guilty party and bring him to justice. Bucher's my best lead. I'm just sorry Louella showed up right now."

"If he is the counterfeiter his daughter arrived at the wrong time. Is she staying with him out there?"

"For the moment. She left her bags in my room just in case."

"In case of what?"

"Come on, Weschcke. She hasn't seen him for six years, and didn't know what his reaction would be."

"That's understandable. But Spur, go slow. Bucher's a mean sonofabitch. He comes into town once in a while to buy supplies, and when his horse hits the street the womenfolk—and most of the men—go into hiding."

Spur smiled. "Marshal, I don't scare easily. In fact, I'm thinking of going back out there tonight. Late tonight, to do some checking."

Weschcke sighed. "Best of luck," he said. "But don't get yourself killed."

"I can take care of myself." Spur walked to the door.

"You might want to stop by and talk to Laurel.
She's up the stairs in the saloon. Her office is the
first door to the right on the landing."

"Thanks," Spur said.

"I just can't get over how much you've
changed, Louella," Emil Bucher said as he
watched his daughter slicing potatoes and onions
into the soup stock.

"It has been six years, daddy."

"I know, but—hell, you're a grown woman!"
He blanched. "Sorry about my language, Louella.
I haven't had any womenfolk around to keep me
in line."

"That's okay." Louella concentrated on her
work, pouring out her frustrations on the potato.
She wished her father would leave her alone. How
stupid of me, she berated herself. I never should
have left Philadelphia!

"You want some help with that?" Bucher asked
as he stubbed out his cigarette in a cracked
porcelain cup.

"No thanks, Daddy."

There was an awkward silence.

"Well, make yourself comfortable—if you can.
Haven't cleaned up this place since—I guess I
never have." He laughed shortly.

"That's okay. After lunch I'll see what I can do
to help straighten things up." She kept her gaze
riveted on the greasy wall.

"I guess I should be checking on the cattle."
He stood to leave.

"I'll call you when lunch is ready," Louella
said. Then with an effort, turned and smiled at

him over her shoulder.

"Fine. And Louella, it is good to see you again." He nearly went to her, arms outstretched, then he slammed them down to his sides and walked out the kitchen door.

Relieved, Louella sliced the potatoes savagely. Each greyish-white cube dropped solidly into the water in the pot, splashing it up onto the stove top, where it sputtered in the flames from the wood fire below the cauldron.

How'd I never let Spur talk me into coming? Louella wondered silently. I knew I should have left town on the first stage coach that passed through. Look at the situation you've gotten yourself into, Louella Bucher. Just look at it!

Her father had been tentative all morning, choosing his words carefully, measuring each emotion before he showed it to her. The pauses in their conversation and her father's averted eyes were driving her crazy. She'd been much better off in Philadelphia. At least there she'd been bored and unhappy in glittering surroundings, meeting interesting men and often having fun with them behind her aunt's back. But here—

Louella threw the rest of the potato into the pot of simmering water. It splashed out and doused the fire below it. Louella laughed and turned to look around the kitchen.

It, like the rest of the house, was a dump. Bags of rotting potatoes crowded the floor, unwashed dishes were stacked everywhere. Empty cans and stains covered the bare wood floor.

Her father was a miserable failure at ranching,

she knew. Proberly worse than anyone in Caliente had told her. He must just be getting by.

When she'd broached the subject of the ranch-house's condition he'd told her that, since there weren't any women around, except an old squaw that came in to cook every once in a while, he'd never wasted any of his hard earned cash "prettifying" the place. If he'd known Louella was coming out there she might have found things radically different.

Louella hugged herself for a moment, then yelped as she backed her rear end against the still warm stove. She had to get out of there. How could she politely tell her father she wanted to leave? And would he let her go?

For the hundredth time that morning Louella wished she hadn't let Spur McCoy ride off. Not that she needed his protection—she felt safe enough with her father, if uneasy. And she could probably find her way back to Caliente—she'd watched the route they'd taken and had tried to remember landmarks and trails—but it would be hard.

Then she brightened. Her bags! They were still in Spur's room in Caliente. She could tell her father she had to return to town to pick them up, then take the first stage back to the village of Los Angeles, then the train back up to San Francisco, and then home.

That would be her excuse, Louella Bucher thought, as she looked down at the cooling soup. She bent to open the firebox and cleaned up the wet ashes inside it, longing for the moment she could ride out, leaving her father behind her forever.

"Can I help you? And I certainly hope so," the grey-haired lady asked Spur as he stepped into Laurel's office above the saloon. Rich oak panelling covered the walls, and crushed red velvet curtains flanked the huge windows. Crystal candle scounces were placed at five foot intervals along the walls. "My, I can tell you're not from around here. Caliente doesn't grow men as handsome as you." She rose from her ornate desk and moved gracefully toward him, her green satin dress rustling as she walked. Laurel extended a gloved hand.

Spur took it and kissed it gently. "I hope you can help me."

"Whatever you want, you've got, mister. Why go all the way to San Diego when you can have the girl of your dreams right here in Caliente?" She smiled invitingly.

"That's not why I'm here."

"Oh." Her smile faded. "You sure about that?"

"Yes. The name's Spur McCoy. You being a business woman, I'm sure you'll understand that what I have to say to you is confidential."

The woman eyed him curiously. "I can keep a secret," she said. "Lots of them. Hell, it's my job!"

"Good. I'm here in town investigating the counterfeit twenty dollar gold pieces that have been showing up in the area. Marshal Weschcke told me one of your girls got paid one last night."

"Yes, damnit," she said, irritated. She dropped the gracious hostess act. "Take a seat, McCoy," the elderly woman said, pointing to a velvet covered wooden chair.

"Thanks." He sat gingerly in the luxurious chair.

"I can't believe it. I told my girls to be careful after hearing poor old Don Arturo got some of those phony double-eagles, but Deborah was so dazzled by the twenty dollars her customer handed her that she just didn't think. As soon as I saw it we went out and looked around for the man but he was gone. Not many places to hide in this town."

"Did you see him?"

"Sure. My door was open, like it always is, and I saw him pass by with Deborah. Have to check up on the girls so they pay me fairly. But I didn't get more than a glance at him."

"Could you describe him to me?"

Laurel shook her head. "Nope. He was short, that's about all I remember. And Deborah said he wasn't much in the meat department, if you catch my meaning.," She smiled savagely. "Serves that dishonest bastard right, having a tiny dick."

"Is Deborah here? Can I talk to her?"

"Sorry, Mr. McCoy. After last night she up and quit the business—at least she left for San Diego this morning with some yahoo who promised to marry her. She'd heard the story a thousand times before, but after that asshole—pardon my French—cheated her she just didn't have the heart to go on." The woman fanned herself with a delicate hand.

Spur nodded. "That happens." He stood.

"I hope you find the bastard who cheated me!" Her pupils narrowed. "I've been in business for thirty years—started in New York, then St. Louis. Moved to San Fransisco but it was too damp there. Made my arthritis flare something fierce. I worked my way down to San Diego, where there was too much competition in the Stingaree, and finally settled here. And in all that time I never had a customer leave without paying fair and square." She looked him up and down. "And by the way, I'm always looking for new customers—especially repeats."

Spur rose to leave.

The elderly woman studied his crotch and smiled. "Looks like you're well equipped to love women. You know how to use that weapon?"

"I do my best," Spur said.

She smiled appreciatively. "How big is that damned thing when it gets angry? Ten inches, eleven?"

"Something like that. Don't really know."

"Hell, business's slow today, like it always is. How about you going on into one of the rooms and having a little fun? No charge—I never charge lawmen."

"Who said I was a lawman?" Spur asked.

"Well, I—" Laurel smiled. "Look, McCoy, you can keep your little secrets, and I'll keep them too. But if some night you need a girl to keep you warm, you just come on up here and I'll fix you up right nice."

"Thanks, Laurel," Spur said.

"No charge. Never a charge for a lawman!"

Spur heard her laughter as he walked down the stairs.

15

Spur spent the rest of the day in his hotel room, thinking about the facts at hand, going over and over it in his mind until he'd come to one inescapable conclusion.

Emil Bucher was his only suspect.

But, though everything pointed to him, McCoy didn't have a shred of evidence supporting his suspicions. He hoped to change that this evening when he rode out to Bucher's ranch for a little nosing around.

Spur checked with the hotel manager but Louella hadn't returned to Caliente that day. He worried about the young woman, thrust into an unpleasant situation with her father, who just might be the criminal he was looking for.

At least he hadn't told Louella the real reason he was in Caliente—not that he didn't trust her, but because he certainly didn't want Bucher to

know he was investigating the counterfeit coins.
Bucher, or anyone else who might possibly be
involved.

But someone knew—or, at least, someone was
worried enough about Spur to send a man to kill
him. He figured the black who attacked him
hadn't been robbing his room. It seemed he'd
been there for one reason.

Yes, Spur told himself, it had to be Bucher. The
Indian had worked for him, at least one Indian
had; a short man also worked for him, and for all
he knew Bucher probably also had a black hand
as well.

Now he only had to get proof—supporting his
theory or disproving it. If Bucher wasn't the man
he'd have to start over.

There were the Chaters, but they seemed
reasonable people. Weschcke had said that no one
who came regularly to town would even consider
passing phony twenty dollar gold pieces there,
and that seemed right. Of course, the Indian
might have gotten the coins from elsewhere and
spent them here, but the two that had turned up
last night seemed to kill that idea.

No. The counterfeiter was nearby.

At dusk, after supper, Spur started to leave his
room, then glanced at the rifle standing in the
corner. Might as well take it—it might come in
handy.

After buying some rounds at the general store
Spur walked slowly down the two block long
street, nodding to the few other people he saw.

Twenty yards later, when he was still a block

from the livery stables, Spur sensed someone following him. He quickly but nonchalantly turned, leaned against a post, and started whistling.

No one around that looked suspicious, Spur quickly thought. He looked at the dark alleys that ran between the buildings. Anyone following him could have ducked into one of them, possibly without his seeing him.

Spur shrugged and moved on toward the stables, this time checking with his peripheral vision. A blur of movement across the street made his head turn, but again he saw nothing but Laurel, the madam, who waved blithely to him as she walked by.

You're letting the job get to you, Spur chided himself.

Then it happened again. He detected a flash of movement in the corner of his left eye. Fuck this, Spur thought, and dashed around the corner of a two story frame house. Might as well hurry things along.

He slapped up against the wall, holding the rifle pressed to his chest, waiting.

Five seconds. Ten seconds. Nothing.

Come on, Spur thought. I know I wasn't imagining that. Show yourself!

A man rushed into the alley. Spur swung up the Spencer to blast him into the next world, then stopped when he saw the huge white beard.

"Weschcke, what the hell are you doing?" he asked gruffly, lowering the weapon. "You almost got yourself killed!"

The town marshal puffed. "Hell, I was just about to ask you the same question. You havin' some kind of trouble? I saw you acting a little strange out on the street, so I thought I'd come by and see if you needed any help."

"Thanks, but no thanks," Spur said. "Someone's following me. Just keep up against the wall."

"Okay."

A split second later a rifle discharged somewhere across the street and a flame of pain burned out across Spur's upper left arm. The two men dropped to the ground as a woman screamed somewhere nearby.

"You okay?" Spur asked in a low voice.

"Yeah. That was close," Weschcke whispered.

"Too close." McCoy ignored the wound, knowing from experience that it wasn't bad, and searched the street. Two alleys had clear lines of sight to his position. No movement, no more gunfire, nothing.

Then he saw the light of a second story room illuminating a white cloud of smoke. That's the alley, Spur thought.

He sent two shots into the area but knew as he returned fire that he had no target. Might as well not waste good ammunition, he thought, and held off firing.

"See anyone?" Weschcke asked.

"No. I'm going over there."

Weschcke produced a six-shooter. "I'll cover," he said.

Spur darted behind a water barrel sitting on the

edge of the boardwalk. Nothing from the alley. Two men stumbled out of the saloon and loudly asked what was happening.

He peppered the alley again with two shots, quickly reloaded, and dropped to his belly on the street.

Nothing.

McCoy jumped to his feet and charged the dark walkway between the buildings, moving fearlessly into the shadows, and found nothing but the dusty ground.

Spur raced to the other side of the alley, then surveyed the area. Back doors of businesses and houses on the street stretched down the block. Half the doors lay open and probably none of them was locked. A cloud blocked the moon's light and beyond a few yards the ground was solidly black.

His assailant had probably saddled up and ridden off by then, Spur thought, and turned toward the street.

He darted around, ducking down alleys, checking stores, but saw no one acting strangely.

"Anything?" Weschcke asked as Spur walked back to him.

"No. Didn't see him, damnit!"

"Wonder if that was the black man who tried to plug you earlier."

"Maybe. Don't know. Think I'll head over to Bucher's place early," Spur said. "Maybe I can find out something while they're still awake. Besides, it's probably safer for me there than in town."

"Probably."

The two men moved into a pool of light from the saloon.

"McCoy, you're hit!" Weschcke said, touching the man's arm below the seared, blood-soaked area.

Spur frowned. In all the excitement he'd forgotten about it.

"Come on to the office and let me have a look at that," Weschcke said. "I've done my share of doctorin' out here."

"I'm fine," Spur said.

"Sure. But might as well check it just in case."

The pain flared up and Spur nodded.

Two minutes later Weschcke rolled up McCoy's left sleeve and inspected the wound. Gunpowder mixed into the edges of the long, angry red scar. "Just a graze," he said, grabbing a bottle of whiskey.

"Thought so. Didn't feel like it'd smashed into anything vital."

"This won't take a minute," he said, and splashed the liquor onto the wound.

Spur winced at the increased pain. "Hurry up, Weschcke. I'm wasting valuable time." The alcohol burned the wound, killing any germs.

"Ain't nothin' out there at Bucher's spread that can't wait another minute," he said, grabbing a roll of gauze from his desk drawer. He tore off a yard of it, then wrapped it tightly around Spur's wound. The marshal split the end and tied the bandage securely. "That should hold you for now."

"Thanks, doc," Spur said, and left for his horse.

"Concha! I can't go any faster!" Lupe Guerra said in Spanish as the twins rode home in their carriage. They'd spent the day in Caliente shopping.

"I knew that if you looked through every bolt of cloth we wouldn't get home in time for supper. Now it's dark. What will papa say?"

Lupe smirked in the thin moonlight. "What will papa say?" she mocked. "What he always says, how we're bad girls and he doesn't know what he did to God to deserve us," Lupe said, and laughed. "And then he'll kiss our foreheads and send us to bed. Hopefully not alone."

Concha shook her head, ignoring the lusty remark. "You know it isn't safe out here, not for two girls all alone at night. *Anything* could happen to us."

Lupe threw her head back. "I bet you're hoping anything will happen." She laughed musically. "Don't worry. We can watch out for ourselves."

"I know, but—"

"Concha, you're making the horses nervous."

The two geldings walked along at a normal rate, heads held still, but Concha inspected them closely.

"Come on, Lupe, give me the reins. Only I know how to make those horses fly." She reached for them.

Lupe gently shouldered her sister back to her side of the carriage seat as she held her hands out of reach. "Relax, sister. Soon we'll be home and you'll be complaining about something else."

"I don't complain!" Concha shrieked.

"Concha, the horses!" Lupe hushed her and, smiling, continued driving into the darkness.

Shit. Fuck!

Shorty Palmer rode slowly back to the ranch, then turned his mount and headed back to town for a minute. Confused, he reined her in and sat motionless.

Shorty couldn't face Bucher again, not after having failed to kill Spur a second time.

What was he going to do?

Shorty had waited around the outskirts of Caliente all day, moving his position at hourly intervals, waiting for dusk. Then he'd spotted the man and tried to hide while following him, but McCoy had seen him and ducked into an alley. He knew he had only one good chance at slamming some rounds into the man but he hadn't compensated for the distance and the shot went high. Hell, he didn't even know if he hit the man or not.

Damn.

As he sat there, wondering what to do, Shorty heard a carriage approaching nearby. He rode quietly to the spot where he figured he'd intercept the vehicle and waited.

As it came into view Shorty saw two bonneted figures riding in it. Women, he thought, and salivated.

He knew he couldn't go back to the whorehouse in Caliente, probably ever. That Indian girl he'd raped in the morning had been fun, but the more Shorty got, the more he wanted it.

Besides, this might be his last chance to get a little pussy, he thought.

As the carriage started to pass by Shorty rolled from the horse and hit the soft ground, moaning as if in pain.

"Lupe!" a girl's voice said from the carraige. "*Alto!*"

From his position Shorty couldn't see the carriage but heard it stop, then boots scraping along the ground, approaching him.

He groaned again and twisted on the dirt.

"Are you hurt?" A Latin-accented voice said.

He nodded, not looking up at her. Christ, he thought, let her be pretty.

"Concha, what is it?" The second voice was farther away, on the carriage.

"*Hombre,*" she said.

"I figured it was a man," she answered in Spanish. "What's wrong with him?"

"I—I don't know, Lupe. *Senor,* what hurts?" Concha asked, bending over him.

"My cock." Shorty grabbed the Spanish girl and wrestled her to the ground. "You and me are gonna have a little fun, *amigo.*"

"*Que?*" Lupe asked.

Concha screamed.

"And your friend's invited along!" Shorty got to his knees above the resisting girl.

"*Estupido homre,*" Lupe said.

Shorty looked up at the second girl, then frowned as he saw the rifle's barrel of death glinting in the moonlight as it pointed at his head. The girl held the rifle with a steady, determined grip.

Concha slapped his face with one hand, slid his gun from his holster, kneed his stomach and scrambled out from beneath him. She ran to the man's horse and unslung the rifle from it, then, pushing the six-shooter down into her bodice, leveled the rifle at the man on the ground.

"Hey, look, little ladies," Shorty said, dazed by the sudden turn of events. "I was just out for a little fun. You—you're not gonna use those things on me, are you?"

"Bastard!" Lupe spat. "How *dare* you attack us! You picked the wrong girls! Our father taught us how to shoot!'"

"Now look!" he said, still hoping he could talk them out of it. "Can't we—"

"Go ahead, Lupe," Concha said. "Kill him. That way he won't be able to attack any other poor, defenseless girls!" She squealed in excitement.

"Shit, ladies, I didn't mean nothin'. I wasn't gonna hurt you, just have a little—"

Lupe fired two rounds a foot above his head.

Shorty felt his urine soak his crotch and run down his thighs.

"Get on your horse and ride out of here before we blow your thing off!" Concha screamed.

Palmer sighed and stood, glad the women couldn't tell he'd pissed in his pants.

"Faster!" Lupe said.

As he ran to his horse the two women blasted

rounds into the ground at his feet.

"Shit, ladies, no hard feelin's, okay?"

"Git!"

Enraged, Shorty rode away as fast as he could, the unfamiliar mount fighting him. As he rode he heard high Mexican laughter filtering through the night air.

16

"You should be married, you know," Emil Bucher said across the table as he ate the simple supper of creamed corn, steak, mashed potatoes and rolls that his daughter had prepared for him.

"I'm a grown woman, Father. I can do what I like." Louella put down her fork. She couldn't put up with this for much longer. He was sounding more like his maiden sister every minute, always nagging.

"You're still my daughter, or has six years of high living changed that?" His voice rose.

"No, of course not." She kept her voice gentle to hide the feelings boiling up inside her.

"Then you better listen to what I say!" he said flatly, and stuffed a forkful of mashed potatoes into his mouth. "We'll get you married off as soon as possible."

"I'd rather not talk about it, Father." She

171

pushed away her plate. Her head pounded.

"If you're gonna hang around here you'd better get used to talking about it! Hell, I can't afford to support you while you grow old alone."

She glanced at him sharply. "That's not what you said in your last letter to me."

"Louella, I—"

"You lied to me!" She stood and paced the kitchen. "You said this ranch was prospering, that you were making more money than you could possibly spend. Where is it? It's not here, and you certainly are not making it on this ranch. Why couldn't you be honest with me?"

"Hell, Louella, I didn't want you to worry. Now I'm sorry I ever thought about your feelings."

"My feelings! You think I wouldn't want to know the truth? All you had to do was send a telegram to Aunt Agnes. She would've sent you money if you'd just asked her. You know how well off she is."

He scowled, slamming his fork down onto the tin plate. "Hell, I wouldn't take a cent from that damned woman if she came here and delivered it in person." Bucher stood. "I never should have left you with Agnes. She's changed you into a headstrong, spoiled little brat who thinks she deserves to have everything she wants!"

Louella laughed. "You don't know what you're talking about. I was practically her prisoner. She watched me day and night, forced me to go to all these boring balls and dinners. I'm not a spoiled little brat!"

"So you got soft, did you? Didn't appreciate

what you had? Look at me when I speak to you, Louella!''

She turned violently toward him. "So I'm looking," she said sarcastically. "And I don't like what I see. You've changed too, Father. You're even worse than you were before you came out here. You're a loud mouthed monster, lacking any kind of feelings at all except hate and anger!''

"All right, yeah, I am bitter. Why the hell shouldn't I be? After my poor Louise died for nothing, for no good reason? Shouldn't that make a man bitter?'' He approached her.

"For a while, yes, but forever? I got over Momma's death. Sure, it took a while, a few years. It hurt badly. But I did it. And you can too.''

He snorted. "Easy for you to say, girl.''

"I am not a girl, Louella said, tossing her head. "I'm a grown woman.''

He paused. "You still a *virgin* grown woman?''

She looked at him in pretended shock. "Father, how could you ask me such a question?''

"Well, are you? Answer me!''

Louella lifted her right eyebrow. "It's none of your damned business. When you left me to come out to this dump you gave up the right to ask me that.''

He grimaced. "You aren't, are you?''

"I told you, Father, it's none of your business.''

A cloud passed over Bucher's face. "Bet you've been screwing every man that comes along. Huh?''

Louella couldn't push down the anger that had

been exploding within her. "All right, Father. Yes, I've been to bed with men," she said, her voice rising. "Every one who happened along! But I only drop my dress for real men, not men like you." She paused, waiting for the words to register on her father's face. When his ears started turning red she laughed. "Want to know if I'm any good? Well, I am. Damn good!" She laughed. "Hell, ask Spur McCoy!"

Bucher's eyed widened. He pushed over the wooden table, sending the plates and cups crashing to the floor. Louella jumped back.

"You little hussy!" he screamed. "You gave yourself to that—that spineless shithead?"

"Yes, and I'm glad I did. Not just once, but again and again. And every time it was better. He rode me until we were both raw. You don't believe me? Ask him the next time you see him. Go on, ask him!"

"Shut your mouth, cunt! You gotta lotta nerve coming here and parading around your sins!"

"*My* sins? I heard in town that you were screwing some old, ugly Indian woman morning, noon and night! Is that how you try to block out the pain of Mother's death? Is that how you're showing your grief?"

"Bitch!" he screamed, kicking a pot across the floor as he walked to her, hand upraised.

"If you touch me—" she warned.

"You'll what?" Bucher said, lowering his hand. His eyes clouded with doubt.

"I'll—I'll—"

Bucher wiped his sweaty forehead and was

silent for a minute. When he spoke again he was calmer, but still boiling. "Look, Louella, I don't give a shit about what you've done in the past— not even your taking that damned McCoy's dick in your hole. Just don't talk about it, girl! Don't make me mad. I don't know what I'll do to you if you make me mad again!"

Louella straightened her shoulders. Her cheeks burned with anger. "So it's okay for you to make me mad, not the other way around? Fine. I'll spend the night in this—this—hellhole, but first thing in the morning I'm leaving here and never coming back!"

"Good! You couldn't do anything that would make me happier!" Emil Bucher walked to the door, the underarms of his shirt soaked with perspiration. "You never should have come here, Louella. Especially now."

"I know!" she yelled.

Bucher stormed out of the room.

Louella sighed and looked at the mess on the floor. In the dirty kitchen it hardly showed at all.

A minute later, Bucher walked into the barn, closed the door behind him, lit a lantern and went to the safe. Kneeling on the straw colored dirt he quickly dialed the combination and flipped the door open. Damn that woman! he thought, pulling two saddle bags of completed counterfeit coins from the safe. That little bitch really got him angry.

Still, he'd done what he'd set out to do. Hell, he'd made her so mad she'd definitely leave in the morning, like she said she would. Once Louella was out of his hair Bucher could get on with his business.

At first he thought he'd have to fake his anger, but when she'd started talking like that—how she'd let all those men use her, and especially that asshole McCoy—the feelings just rolled off him. He was somewhat surprised she was willing to spend the night, and wished he'd argued with her earlier so she'd be gone by now.

He placed the two saddlebags on the rickety table next to the stamping machine and stove where he melted the gold, then retrieved the lantern from where he'd placed it beside the safe and put it next to the bags.

Bucher spilled out their contents onto the table and looked at them. He was getting closer and closer to the magic number. He breathed hard to calm himself. If he and his men worked day and night—once Louella was out of his hair—he might be able to finish earlier.

Of course, he didn't know how much work he'd get out of Sam Johnson, after the way he'd used him that morning. But it served the damned bastard right, Bucher thought. Hell, he should be glad he was still alive.

Making the coins was a simple process. He had Johnson and Shorty strike the blanks from the base metals. Then he'd melt the free hold he'd found in the hills, coat the blanks, and then re-strike them, carefully positioning the coins so that the second impression laid down perfectly over the first. Most of the coins came out fine, except for the weight. He buried the bad ones, but the weight bothered him. Too late to worry about that now, Bucher thought. It was as close as he could come to the genuine article.

After staring at the gold covered coins he decided he'd better count them all. He got the other bags from the safe and spent a half hour on the project. When he finished he realized he was twelve short—the ten that Lazy Eye had stolen.

And two more.

Damn!

He recounted and came up with the same figures.

One of his men had stolen two more coins. Johnson? Bucher thought and shook his head. No.The black was too yellow to do that. So it had to be Shorty. He'd show that sonofabitch when he came back!

By then, though, Spur McCoy should be dead. That was something to look forward to, hearing that Shorty'd killed the bastard. Right after he heard it Bucher would blow Palmer's brains out.

No. He had to wait until Louella left. In the morning, then, Bucher thought. Hell, he'd have to hire a new hand.

Clouds passed over the moon. After tying his rented horse to a tree nearby, Spur had squatted behind a bush on a hill overlooking Bucher's ranch. He'd been there an hour and had seen nothing suspicious, although a man—perhaps Bucher—had gone into the barn. Seems to be a lot of activity in there, Spur thought, for a non-working ranch.

He heard a horse not far off. Spur faded back into the shadow of an oak tree with a four foot thick trunk and waited. A rider approached.

The horseman paused ten feet from him. Spur saw his silhouette, lighter than the darkness behind him, in the intermittent moonlight. No way to tell who he was, McCoy thought.

The man reached into his vest pocket and pulled out a bag of makings. Less than a minute later, as Spur stood absolutely still in the shadows nearby, the figure stuck the cigarette into his mouth and struck a light.

A black man. Spur was sure he recognized him as the one who'd broken into his room. The man's face, caught in the glow of the sulphur match, electrified McCoy into action.

He ran three paces and, taking a quick jump, smashed his whole two hundred pounds against the man's side.

The horse whinneyed and shot forward as the black fell to the ground with Spur on top of him.

"What the—"

Spur slammed his Bowie knife into the man's chest, piercing his heart. He clamped a hand down over the man's mouth to stifle his screams and twisted the blade savagely, then ripped it out and slashed his throat.

The man died silently seconds later, his last breath bubbling out through his opened windpipe as his blood pump ceased to function.

Spur wiped the blade on the ground, stuck it into the sheath hanging from his belt, and walked

slowly to the dead man's horse, which had
stopped a few yards away.

"Easy, girl, easy," he said, taking its reins.
McCoy led the skitterish beast to a tree where he
tied it securely. No sense in alerting Bucher to his
presence.

Spur returned to his hiding place in time to see
the figure leave the barn and return to the house.
Must be Bucher, he thought.

It might be worthwhile checking out the barn
while it was empty. Could be interesting. After
waiting a few minutes he walked toward the edge
of the hill.

Time to move.

"Father! Come in here!" Louella screamed.

Seconds later Bucher banged the door open and
stormed into the house. "Don't you ever shut up?
What the fuck is it, bitch? I'm busy."

Be firm, Louella reminded herself. She looked
him squarely in the eyes. "I've decided I can't
spend another minute here."

"Yeah?' Bucher said, and laughed.

"That's right," Louella said in her darkest
voice. "Get me a horse. I'm riding out tonight!"

He smiled. "No way I'll let you do that—much
as I'd like to. If you went and got yourself killed
by some drunk bandit I'd never forgive myself.
You know it's not safe for a woman to ride alone
at night."

"I don't care!" she wailed.

He shook his head. "Shit, despite our differ-
ences, how's one night gonna hurt you? Use your

pretty little brain. Come on, girl; did you lose your sense when you lost your cherry?"

"Come with me," Louella said, ignoring her father's remark. She didn't like the idea but it was better than her only alternative.

"I'm too busy."

"Then send one of your men with me. I'm not spending the night in this madhouse!"

"I got work to do." He looked at the door.

"What's more important—getting rid of me or finishing your work?" Louella asked hotly. She wouldn't back out now. Not this time.

"Louella, shut the fuck up." Bucher's voice lowered in volume but doubled in intensity. "Shut your slut-yap and let me get back to my work."

"No!" she said. "I'm leaving. Right now!" Louella walked to the door.

Her father grabbed her arm. "You're not going anywhere, girl."

"Let me go!" she screamed. "You're hurting me!"

Bucher slapped her cheek viciously, then backhanded it again. "Hell, maybe I should let you go get yourself killed. At least I wouldn't have to listen to you screaming anymore. Christ, you sound like a dying cat!" He slapped her again for good measure.

Louella reeled in pain and shock. "You bastard!" She punched his stomach and twisted her arms, attempting to free them from her father's iron grip.

"No. I can't let you do it. You're goin' to bed

and you'll stay there until I say so, slut! You remember beds, don't you? Sure you do. You've been in enough of them!"

"No!" she said again.

Bucher wrestled his daughter toward the single bedroom. "Sleep it off, whore!" he said, pushing her into the room and slamming the door shut.

Louella hit the floor. Surprise, anger, pain and fear mixed in her, producing a deadly combination. She charged to her feet and tried the door knob. It had no lock.

Pressing her ear against it she heard the kitchen door open. Good, at least he's left, Louella thought. She rubbed her stinging cheek and stood, wondering what to do next.

He was right. She couldn't ride in the night for over an hour and reasonably expect to make it to Caliente all alone. Finally she grabbed a rifle from the rack beside the crumbling fireplace and returned to the room. After sitting on the bed she pointed the weapon at the door with timid but determined hands.

I'm ready for you, Louella Bucher thought, and waited for her father's return.

17

As Louella sat on the hard bed, her father's rifle lying across her knees, she sighed and wished, for the thousandth time, that she'd never gotten on that train in Philadelphia, starting the journey which eventually ended in Caliente.

Thinking back, the city hadn't been so bad—certainly not compared with the situation she was now in. Her Aunt Agnes was kind, and really wanted Louella to make something of herself—if only a faithful wife to a rich, older man.

Louella wanted that too, for a while. But as soon as she'd allowed herself to discover the joys of sex, though, that was no longer enough.

The young woman sighed. Those had been exciting, even scary times. Agnes had tried to keep her niece under her thumb, so Louella spent many days thinking up ways to slip out of the house—or even to bring men into her room—

without her aunt's knowledge. The poor old dear would probably die if she knew what Louella did under her roof.

Of course, she didn't always give herself to men there. One time she'd attended a play alone, for her aunt was suffering from influenza and couldn't go. After the curtain calls the dashing leading man had invited her back to his dressing room, where they spent an hour of bliss after the theatre had emptied.

As Louella allowed herself to relive the past the dismal house around her faded and she laid back, clutching the rifle she couldn't shoot, remembering.

Her first time had been one of the best. She was still nineteen, just after her father had left for California. It was a warm summer day and she'd taken a lazy stroll from her aunt's three story brick house down to the creek that meandered behind it, picking wildflowers and then tossing them behind her as she walked.

Louella settled back against the pillow and relived the experience in her mind.

It was a hot summer day and her feet ached. Once at the stream she sat on its grassy banks, slipped off the tight, pearl-buttoned shoes and dangled her feet in the cool water, enjoying the liquid refreshment.

Her aunt's property ended at the stream. A long vacant house stood on the other side, halfway up the hill. She was relaxing in the sun, arching her back and stretching cat-like, when she heard gruff male voices approaching from far off.

Startled, she grabbed her shoes and ran to a clump of five foot high elder trees, four feet from the stream. Louella peered past them, then sucked in her breath.

Two tall, lanky men in their twenties, dressed in nothing but tight yoke-waisted shorts, like her father used to wear around the house in the morning, walked up to the stream. Her throat tightened as she looked at their hairy bodies and brief clothing.

One man, older than the other, punched his companion's shoulder lightly, laughed, and said something that she couldn't remember.

Still talking he casually reached down, unbuttoned his shorts, and lowered them. Louella blushed as he kicked them off and jumped into the river.

She'd never seen a naked man—not even her father, though she'd heard from a girl friend that their bodies were different than women's. Louella had been observant enough to realize this—*something* made men's crotches bulge—but couldn't for the life of her figure out what.

A quick glimpse was all she needed to see to know that she liked men's things, whatever they were.

While the first one splashed around in the waist deep water his friend stripped more slowly. Louella caught her breath as he finally stood naked. It's huge, she thought, staring at the limp cylinder of flesh that hung between his legs.

A dull itch started between her legs, down there, and grew more intense. As she gazed at the man, who stood with his arms crossed on his hairy chest, chatting with his swimming friend, she pressed her hand against her groin and rubbed.

The stifling heat, mixed with the drone of countless insects in the trees around her, nearly made Louella swoon. She leaned against a birch tree that had grown up alongside the elder and pressed her legs together as she continued to rub. The hairy man's organ swayed as he walked along the bank, following his friend. As he grew closer to her on the other side of the stream Louella was fascinated to see two small, dark brown objects swinging and hanging behind his thing.

The rubbing wasn't enough. Thinking she was fairly well hidden, Louella spread her legs, lifted her skirt and petticoats, and reached up beneath them.

She hadn't worn her bloomers that morning, since it had been so hot, and so her fingers quickly contacted her hairy mound. She scratched the lush hairs, then for no reason she could later fathom, pushed a finger up between her legs.

The young girl gasped, then quickly covered her mouth. The men hadn't seemed to notice. Louella pushed three fingers into her cleft. It seemed to hurt at first, then as she gently moved them around shock waves of pleasure melted through her.

After taking one last look at the naked man now rapidly drawing nearer to her Louella closed her eyes, wrapped up on the new sensations flooding through her. She'd never touched herself down there, not even while bathing, and the sensations were mind-boggling.

The men's voices grew louder, as did the sounds of splashing, as she explored and delighted in this taboo, dirty, sinful part of her body. She probed and rubbed and spread her lips, lost in sensation, for several minutes. It was like nothing she'd ever felt before.

A sharp laugh from nearby reminded her that she wasn't alone. Louella opened her eyes quickly and saw the hairy man standing directly across the river from her, staring.

Blushing, she pulled her hand from her crotch— then gaped. The man's organ was growing, stiffening, lengthening until it was at least three times as large as it had been previously. Soon, as she looked on with amazement, it jutted up hard, gleaming in the harsh sunlight, its flared head nearly touching the man's belly.

Louella knew she should run, or be embarrassed, or something, but she couldn't stop staring.

"My lady, do you want some company?" the man with the erection asked.

She looked up at his face, blanched, started to rush toward the house, then sighed and slowly nodded.

He laughed shortly. "Get on back to work, Jason," he said. "This little filly's mine!"

The other man. She'd forgotten him! Louella turned in time to see Jason, sporting a man-thing in the same condition, nod and walk to retrieve his shorts.

As she brushed her skirts down the man walked

across the stream, his organ bobbing as he took
three great strides and then walked to within six
feet of the young girl. Her mouth opened as she
stared.

"You like what you see, don't you?" he asked,
his black eyes sparkling.

Louella nodded again, leaning further back
against the tree.

"I like what I saw—you playing with yourself."

"What—what is that?" Louella blurted out,
pointing toward his crotch.

He put his hands on his hips, threw his head
back and laughed loudly, accentuating his endow-
ment.

"No, tell me, please," Louella said. "I—I've
never seen one."

He stopped then, his lips parted, then
shrugged. "It's—it's where a man lives," he said,
and walked closer, stopping three feet from the
girl. "It's where a woman lives too."

"But what's it called?" Louella asked, almost
reaching out for it.

"God, girl, you are green!" He took her
hesitant hand and wrapped her fingers around it.
Bending close to her ear, he whispered, "That's
my cock."

It was alive inside her fingers. Warm, hard, yet
soft, pulsing with a life all of its own. As she
squeezed it experimentally Louella felt the
burning between her legs again.

"Well, what—what do you do with it?" she
blurted.

The man smiled. "Lots of things. I piss with it,

pull it off on lonely, cold nights—and pleasure ladies. That's the best of all."

"Pleasure ladies?" Louella asked.

He nodded, then grinned. "Let me show you."

She allowed the man to undress her, unashamed, for he was already naked, spectacularly so, and she felt it was a fair trade.

As she sat on the grass he unbuttoned her shoes, pulled them off, and helped her to stand. Her dress went next, then her chemise. As her youthful, white breasts were exposed he whistled.

"Nice tits," he said, then squatted and lowered her petticoats. "Christ." He touched her fur patch, then pushed his nose against it and sniffed. "Girl smell," he muttered.

"That itches," Louella said, pushing against his hand. She knew she should be shocked, humiliated, struck by lightning. Instead she was glowing, soothed, at peace as the man rose before her.

"I can take care of that." He moved his hand away.

"With your—cock?" Louella hazarded.

He smiled. "See? You're learning fast." He lowered her to her knees on the grass and stood in front of her, his crotch directly before her. "Put your face near it," he whispered, guiding her head with gentle hands.

Louella sighed as she bent forward, toward his magnificent penis. Her mouth watered.

"Smell it. Taste it," he said.

Louella hesitated, then yielded to the gentle pressure of his hands and pushed her nose against it. The throbbing deep inside her increased as she inhaled his musk, then nuzzled the coarse, dark brown hairs and closely inspected the fleshy globes.

He gripped it at its base and, moving back her head, ran the red head of it over her lips several times. She opened her mouth, suddenly desperate to experience this man any way she could.

"Suck it," he said. "Go on. Like a candy pop." He pushed it between her parted lips.

Louella's nostrils flared as he moved the huge, red head into her mouth. She started to gag, but moaned as the man moved his foot up between her legs and massaged her opening.

As she looked up at him the man slipped several inches of his penis into her mouth, pumped a few times, then pulled out. He chuckled and stood there, looking down at her tenderly, as the tip of his erection glistened with her saliva.

"No you don't! I'm not gonna waste my seed there." He pushed her to the ground, spread her legs, and laid on top of her. "Just relax," he said, his face inches from hers.

With his warm breath soothing against her the man reached down and guided his organ to her opening. Louella gasped as he began to slide into her. He grunted twice, frustrated, then finally pushed past the last barrier and rammed home.

The girl clawed his back and then clung to him. "You like that, don't you?" he asked as he began thrusting.

Louella's thoughts and words were lost in a sea of new sensations as the man stroked harder into her. He closed his eyes and pushed his tongue into her mouth. Louella sucked it in, tears forming in her eyes, as his constant movement sent chills through her.

"Oh God!" she said, pulling her mouth from his. "What's this called?" she gasped.

"Fucking," he hissed, pumping harder.

"Fuck me!" Louella groaned. "Fuck me with your cock!"

The man grunted, raised himself off her, then took her right nipple in his mouth. He gently bit and gnawed at the tender flesh, then sucked her whole breast into his mouth as Louella shut her eyes.

The combined sensations were too much. She was going to pass out, Louella thought. It was too much, too much, too—

Her body shook violently beneath the pumping man, blinding her, dazzling her until all she could see were the coal-black eyes of the man sweating above her.

"Help!" she yelled.

He smiled. "Wait until you feel this." He lifted her legs and held them straight up, laid them against his shoulders, then pushed even deeper into her, touching new areas of sensitivity.

Louella shook through another moment of bliss as droplets of sweat rolled off his chest and rained down onto her. He grunted, blowing out his breath in puffs, and smiling reassuringly. Gasping after her second pleasure Louella stared up at him in wonder as his thrusts became erratic, wild.

His face screwed up, his eyes slammed shut and the cords on his neck stood out. He roared uncontrollably, slamming into her so hard it took her breath away, hurting her, then sending her over • the brink a third time.

He crashed down on top of her, all muscle and hair and steaming flesh. His hot breath shot across her ear as he halted deep inside her and wrapped his arms around her body.

They lay like that for a while in the sun, bodies pressed together, connected. Louella kissed his arm as she clutched him, enjoying his weight, his smell, his—his cock still inside, she thought.

He finally lifted his head, smiled, kissed her ear, and pulled out of her. The man sat back on his heels, limp, spent, satisfied.

"That's fucking," he said gently, "and that's what men and women do together. I would say it's way past time you learned."

Louella looked at him. "Thank you," she said, touching his organ. "Thank you very, very much!"

That afternoon was the start of a long career—many men had shared her bed, her body, her secrets, but few had penetrated her heart. Her cheeks burned as she remembered the experience, recalling his face, his taste, his smell. She longed to go back to that kind of life.

As she glanced around the dismal, dirty room on her father's ranch, Louella wished she was once again in the arms of that nameless man, enjoying his body, giving herself willingly, and shamelessly, and, yes, lovingly.

18

A lone figure rode quietly across the landscape. Shorty Palmer moved through the pitch-black shadows that stretched from the massive boulders looming up on either side of the trail.

As he approached the ranch he'd formulated a plan of action. Shorty knew he could never face Bucher again. McCoy was still alive and breathing, as much as he'd tried to change that, and his boss wouldn't accept an excuse. He shuddered as he thought of what the man had done to Johnson. He'd get worse. Bucher'd probably kill him, no questions asked.

Shorty wouldn't even be able to defend himself. Shame flooded through him as he remembered the Mexican girls who'd unarmed him, made him piss his pants, and sent him off on his horse as they laughed at him.

No time for that, he thought, shaking off the

feelings. All he could do was run. First, he needed a weapon. Shorty remembered the old but operational pistol that Johnson kept hanging from his bunk "for emergencies." That would do. Then, he'd change his pants, steal as many of the coins as he could find, and head out tonight—without facing Bucher, if at all possible.

The man frowned. Suppose the coins were locked up in the safe, like they usually were at night? If so, he'd just leave anyway. Better to be broke but alive, Shorty thought, better than dead. Much better!

He tied up the horse he'd borrowed from his employer at the hitching post, listening to shouting coming from the ranchhouse. Bucher and some woman were arguing.

That gave him time. He approached the dark bunkhouse. Was Johnson already snoring away, or was he out on watch? Shorty opened the door. Empty. He squinted through the darkness and smiled. The gun was there.

The man quickly changed into a fresh pair of pants, then strapped on the holster and checked the gun. It was loaded, as always. Next, the coins. He left the bunkhouse and, keeping an eye on the house, walked in through the opened barn doors. He stopped just inside.

A lit lantern sat on the table. In its ring of soft light he saw hundreds of the coins, neatly stacked. Shorty smiled at his good fortune—old Bucher was getting careless.

He quickly scooped up handfuls of the bogus twenty dollar gold pieces and stuffed them into his pockets until they were bulging. As he pushed another handful down the front of his shirt, Shorty heard boots scuffling outside.

Bucher!

Palmer quickly doused the lantern's flame and sank back against the wall, out of the narrow beam of light that shot into the barn from the ranchhouse's windows.

He figured he could kill the old man quickly and easily. Bucher'd be lit up from behind, and Shorty had a clear line of fire. It should be easy, he told himself, as sweat squeezed out on his forehead. All he had to do was wait for the man to walk into his trap.

A minute. Then two.

Where the hell was Bucher?

"Shorty!" he heard his employer call outside. "Damnit, where're you hiding? When I see your ass there'll be hell to pay! You better've killed that damned McCoy!" the man yelled.

Palmer smiled, thinking of how he'd soon be sending the man into Hades. Relax, he thought. You can wait a few more minutes. It would be worth it!

The footsteps died off. Bucher must have noticed that his horse had returned and gone to the bunkhouse looking for him.

He waited, six-shooter in hand, right thumb steady on the trigger. Shorty's right arm was steady as he aimed at the opened twin doors, dreaming of the moment when he would cut the man down and plow him into the ground.

As McCoy made his way gingerly down the hillside the surrounding trees blocked his view of the barn. Great, he thought. Be careful. Bucher might have gone back into the barn in those few minutes.

When he could see the structure again Spur squatted behind a pine and studied it. He remembered seeing a small door in the rear. If it wasn't locked it would be the safest way in—the front doors were too centrally located. If Bucher happened to walk out onto the porch in the next few seconds he'd have a clear view of Spur entering the barn.

McCoy hunched over and cleared the last twenty yards of the hill, then hit flat ground and moved soundlessly to the old, weathered building.

Making absolutely no sound, Spur walked to the small door in the rear. After another look around he pulled firmly on the wrought-iron handle. The door swung open on well greased hinges and he silently slipped inside.

Spur squatted in a shadow. No light inside the barn, save for a bit shining in through the front doors. In the dim glow Spur could make out the shapes of a table, a safe, a stove—and a man leaning against the far wall.

"Bucher?" the figure said uncertainly.

Spur dashed behind some rotting bales of hay as a deadly messenger zinged above his head. He hammered three rounds at the man, but the figure darted to the right just before the heated lead slammed into the barn wall, splintering the dry wood.

The table tipped over as his attacker ducked behind it, sending points of golden light spilling to the floor and clanging dully together.

The counterfeit coins, Spur thought, ducking to avoid another bullet. He had his man. Bucher was the one after all. He quickly pushed four bullets into his .44's chambers, slapped the weapon shut and fired two shots at the table. The wood was thick enough to halt the bullets before they could do any damage.

A round dug into the bale of hay in front of him.

Enough, Spur thought. He dashed to the right of the table, dove onto the ground and fired just as he caught sight of the figure squatting behind the protective wood.

The bullet smashed into the man's chest and jerked him down to the floor. He fired wildly as his body slid four feet until coming to a stop. The labored breathing continued for a few seconds and ended with a long hiss.

Spur rolled behind the old iron safe and waited a minute. When the man hadn't made a move he started to get to his feet.

"What's goin' on here?" Emil Bucher's voice boomed from the barn doors.

Assuming the other man was dead, Spur moved behind the table and crouched next to the body, where he couldn't be seen from the barn doors.

"Palmer, what's going on? Answer me! Did you kill Spur like I told you to? And why're you shooting up the place as if ammo didn't cost good money? You drunk again?"

"Palmer can't answer you," Spur called out, staring down at the shadowy man lying on the

ground beside him. "And no, he didn't kill me."
McCoy checked for the man's pulse but found
none. Good. One down.

"Holy Jesus! That you, McCoy?" Bucher
asked.

Spur watched him through a crack in the two-
inch thick wooden planks. Bucher looked around
the barn, weapon drawn.

"Yes," Spur answered.

The man instantly turned and unloaded his
pistol into the table.

"Emil Bucher, you're under arrest for counterfeiting U.S. currency. Throw down your weapon
and give yourself up," Spur said sternly. It was
worth a try.

"Like hell I will!" he said, and blasted another
shot into the table.

It wobbled a bit but the bullets didn't penetrate
the wood.

"It won't do you any good to kill me, Bucher.
Marshal Weschcke knows I'm here. He's up on
the ridge above the ranch, waiting for my signal.
If you kill me he and his men'll cut you into
pigfood before you have time to spit. Give it up,
Bucher," Spur said.

He laughed. "You got the wrong man."

McCoy watched as he emptied the box of ammo
onto the floor, grabbed the bullets, and reloaded
as he sat behind an oak barrel next to the door.

"I saw the coins. The counterfeit coins you've
been making here?"

"I don't know what you're talking about," the
German yelled. "Come out and let's settle this
right now."

"Forget it, Bucher. Throw down your weapon and show me your hands nice and high."

"No way, McCoy! I'll teach you to mess with me! I knew you were trouble the minute you rode out here. Should've killed you myself. But nothing's gonna stop me from getting my fortune. Not you, not Weschcke, not the whole U.S. Army!"

"You'll never get out of here alive," Spur said, and fired a warning shot. It slammed into the ground a foot from Bucher's right buttock.

The man shifted farther behind the barrel. "And I was worried you might know how to use that thing. Can't you do better than that, McCoy? You shoot worse'n a woman."

"Wise up, you idiot! Hell, I could've killed you dozens of times by now if I wanted to. But I'm giving you a chance to give yourself up. Do it. If not, think about the grave you'll be lying in."

"Go to hell!" the man said.

Spur moved a yard across the floor, dragging the table with him as a shield. "I'm giving you one more chance," he said, sliding the table a bit more to the left. Hot lead slammed into the wood as he repositioned himself.

"Bastard! You think you're gonna kill me!" He fired again. "Damn, that table's thick!"

"So's your head if you think you won't pay for what you've done," the Secret Service man growled. He skidded the table two more yards until he was ten feet from where Bucher crouched behind the barrel. Close enough, Spur thought.

"Get ready to die!" Bucher bellowed, sprang to his feet and blasted his six-shooter.

Spur dropped to his back, bent his knees and slammed the table forward with both feet. It picked up speed as it slid across the slick straw, then banged against the barrel, knocking Bucher's pistol from his hand. The weapon flew ten feet before thudding to the ground.

"Give it up, Bucher."

"I never give up!" he blubbered. The voice was high, tight, uncontrolled.

Spur started to walk toward the gun. "The game's over, Bucher. You're not even armed. Stand up where I can see you."

"What's going on?"

Spur turned and saw Louella Bucher standing in the barn doorway. "Get down!" he yelled.

As he glanced at her Bucher rolled across the floor, grabbed up his gun, and dove back behind the table. "I'm armed now!" he screamed.

Spur ducked behind the stove.

"Spur, is that you?" Louella called.

"Get back to the house, Louella," Bucher roared. "Unless you want to watch me blow your lover-boy's brains all over the floor."

The woman hesitated for a second, then turned to go. The young woman tripped on the slippery straw and fell to the ground with a yelp.

"Damn!" Bucher grabbed her feet and pulled her to him behind the table. "Now you listen real good, McCoy. If you want Louella to live, toss your weapon over here. I don't give a damn about this woman. Hell, she ain't even my daughter! Her mother was knocked up before I ever met her. I felt sorry for Louise so we got married to make things all nice and legal. If you think I won't kill her, you're wrong." He paused, breathing hard. "I'm gonna stand up now. If you shoot you'll blast her into the next world yourself."

The man slowly rose from behind the table, holding the shaking woman around the waist before him. He pressed the muzzle of his six-gun against her forehead.

Spur held his fire. "You're bluffing, Bucher. You'd never kill your own flesh and blood."

Bucher smiled. "You haven't been listening, McCoy. She *ain't* my flesh and blood. So throw your weapon down. Now!" He jabbed the barrel into Louella's skin.

"Spur, I—"

"Shut up!" Bucher screamed. He cocked his weapon with a meaty thumb. "What are you waiting for? Do it!"

A no-win situation, Spur thought, for now. "Convince me," he said flatly.

"Goddamn it! Do I have to blow her head off to make you believe me?"

"You do that and you've lost your ace."

Bucher was confused. "Hell!"

Louella stared at the Secret Service man, her face grim. "Don't do it, Spur. He's lying. I wasn't born until my parents had been married—"

"I told you to shut your yap!" Bucher slapped his right arm over her mouth, retaining his aim but exposing his shoulder.

Spur swung up his six-shooter and peeled off a quickly aimed shot. Louella yelped as the lead dug into Bucher's shoulder, shredding skin, ripping open arteries and shattering bone, before it exited. Bucher screamed but held onto Louella.

"Sonofabitch!" the man blubbered. The wound bled.

"There's no way out, Bucher," Spur said calmly. "Let Louella walk away from you unharmed and you'll live to see sunup. If not—"

As Louella renewed her struggle to free herself of the powerful arm she bent at the waist.

Spur planted a slug into the man's suddenly exposed and vulnerable belly.

Bucher howled in pain as the bullet exploded his vital organs. Louella freed herself and, screaming, dashed outside as her father convulsed, dropping his aim as pain clouded his brain and misted his eyes. The man stumbled forward, shooting wildly and yelling with blood freezing agony.

Spur plowed a slug through the man's heart.

Emil Bucher groaned and fell backward onto the hard packed dirt floor, his chest oozing life. The counterfeiter's booted feet kicked grotesquely for a minute on the straw, then lay still.

As he walked cautiously to the downed man, Spur heard Louella sobbing softly outside. McCoy bent and pulled the pistol from the inert hand, looked down at Bucher one last time, then walked out of the barn.

He found Louella standing in the moonlight hugging herself, her cheeks wet.

"It's over," he said.

19

Louella Bucher stood outside her father's barn, shivering in the cool night air. She was dry-eyed, but stared up at the glowing three quarter moon.

Spur went to her and touched her shoulder.

"I'm sorry, Louella," he said. "I'm sorry you had to find out what kind of man your father was."

The woman turned to him and managed a faint smile. "It's all for the best, I guess. He had changed—more than I could have ever imagined."

"Do you know what was going on here? What your father was doing?"

She shook her head. "No. But I guess I should. How did you get involved with this? Why were you here tonight?"

"I work for the U.S. Government."

"A lawman?" she asked, incredulously.

Spur nodded. "The only reason I came to Caliente was to find out who'd been counterfeiting twenty dollar gold pieces in the area. The first ones turned up almost four weeks ago in town, and I got an assignment to come here and dig out the truth. The man responsible just happened to turn out to be your father."

Louella nodded sadly. "I knew something was wrong here—more than just my father's anger at my coming out here. But it never occurred to me he could be doing something illegal."

"How could you have known? Don't blame yourself," Spur said gently.

"Oh, I don't."

Spur took the woman into his arms.

She looked up at his face. "What happens now?"

Spur glanced back at the barn. "I guess we'll wait until morning and ride into Caliente, then tell Marshal Weschcke what happened here. I probably should go tonight, but I'd hate to leave you here alone."

She shivered visibly. "Thanks. But even with you I don't think I could spend the night here. There's too many bad memories. How long is it until dawn?"

Spur turned uncertainly to the moon, which hung low in the east. "Quite a while, I think."

"Then let's ride back to Caliente right now. Together. Okay? I—I can't stay here much longer."

"Fine. You need to pack anything?"

She shook her head. "I didn't bring much with

me, and I can get it later. Let's just go."

"Where's your coat?" Spur asked gently.

Louella shrugged. "I don't know. It's not that cold out here. Let's just go." She smiled briefly, then bit her lip.

"Sounds fine to me." He kissed her cheek. "I just need to wrap up a few things inside." McCoy nodded to the barn.

"Okay. I'll wait here. But hurry."

Spur found the lantern inside, lit it and took a quick look around the barn. He knelt before the opened safe, reached in—and pulled out two perfect U.S. government-issued double-eagle dies. He whistled and debated a moment, wondering if he should take them with him. He shook his head and slipped them into his shirt for safekeeping. A few small bags were also pushed into the corner of the safe. On opening them and looking inside, Spur whistled. Pure gold, ready for melting. He took the bags with him.

Moving around the barn McCoy also found several saddlebags, and hundreds of counterfeit coins. There were wooden rifle boxes stuffed with thousands of grey colored blank coins, already struck once but which hadn't yet been coated with gold.

After his tour Spur stopped by the door. Bucher lay behind the table, dead, his career in counterfeiting over.

McCoy ran up the hill, retrieved his horse, then led it down to where Louella stood shivering, then got her horse from the hitching post. He helped her onto the saddle, mounted up, and the two of

them left Emil Bucher's ranch behind forever.
Louella didn't look back as they rode out.

After two hours of a slow journey they rode
into Caliente. Spur felt the woman before him
relax as they entered the somewhat familiar surroundings. She leaned back against him and
sighed. Most of the settlement was sleeping. Few
lights shone through windows, save for the lamp
that always seemed to be burning in the town
marshal's office.

After digging the sacks of gold and the dies
from his saddlebags, Spur quickly explained the
situation to Weschcke as Louella waited outside
on the boardwalk.

"Well, I gotta hand it to you, McCoy. You were
right," Weschcke said. "Emil Bucher. Never
would have believed it. How many bodies out
there?"

"Three," Spur said. "Bucher and two of his
hands. One short one, who was probably the one
who gave Laurel's girl a counterfeit coin, and also
the black man who attacked me in my hotel
room."

Weschcke nodded. "Self-defense, I suppose."

"Right."

The town marshal looked at Louella Bucher
outside and lowered his voice. "How's his
daughter takin' it? Must've been quite a shock.
Pretty little thing, too."

"Better than I'd imagined. She understands
what her father was doing, and they've been
separated for so long that she doesn't have any
real feelings left for him. Fortunately she didn't

see me actually killing him, though she heard it all right. That might have been too much for her."

"So you found the dies and the equipment?"

Spur nodded and slapped the bags onto Weschcke's desk. "I took a look around—the dies were in a bag in a small safe in the barn. And there must be at least a thousand of the counterfeit coins lying scattered all over the barn floor. Don't know where he got the gold, but there was prospecting equipment in the barn as well— maybe he made a lucky strike in the hills on his land." Spur opened the bags, revealing the dies and the gold.

Weschcke whistled. "I'll check it out. If Bucher did make a lucky strike I'll use some of the funds from it to pay for decent burials for Bucher and his men, then take care of any taxes on his property. The rest is the woman's. Will she be staying in town?"

"I doubt it, after what happened." He looked at her through the window. "She might go back to Philadelphia. We didn't talk much on the way back here."

Weschcke nodded. "Thanks, McCoy. You did what I obviously couldn't do."

Spur grinned tiredly. "That's my job."

"How's your arm?" Weschcke asked.

He laughed shortly. "In all the excitement I'd forgotten about it. Fine, I guess. Rolled on it a few times but didn't even feel it."

"Good. You get that professionally patched up as soon as you can."

"Will do, Weschcke."

"You'll be in town a few days?"

"At least until tomorrow."

"Then I'll keep the dies in my safe and turn them over to you on your departure."

"Fine. Guess my next stop is San Francisco, to return them to the mint."

The men shook hands, then Spur went out to Louella.

"It's taken care of. Marshal Weschcke will ride out there at first light. We can relax now."

She nodded, silent. Suddenly she turned to him, her eyes anxious in the silver light. "Spur, can we go to bed now?" she asked desperately.

"Sure. I've still got my room. Guess we could both use some sleep."

She shook her head. "That's not exactly what I had in mind. I need something to make me forget what happened out there. And I think you've got just what I need." She pressed her hand against his well stuffed crotch.

Spur turned and saw Weschcke waving to them through the window. They walked to the hotel.

Sunlight spilled into the room as McCoy yawned and stretched, then walked naked to the window and looked out. Caliente hadn't woken up yet, but Spur knew that Weschcke was already out at the dead man's ranch taking care of business.

"Spur, come back to bed," Louella said, brushing the sleep mussed hair from her eyes.

He sat beside her and kissed her cheek. "How

208

you feeling?" he asked gently.

"Fine, I guess." Her breasts glowed in the brilliant sunshine that bounced off the walls and floor. She threw back the sheet and sat, then saw the bandage on his left arm. "Spur! You were hurt! I'm sorry." She bent and kissed the bandage tenderly. "I never even noticed last night."

"You were too busy," he said, smiling. "Just a flesh wound, though. Nothing to worry about."

"It certainly didn't seem to hurt your style yesterday night—or this morning."

"Nope."

She lazily took his limp, spent penis into her hand, stroking it roughly, then tickled his testicles. She pulled gently at the hairs growing there.

"Have you decided what you're going to do next, Louella?" he asked, enjoying her fingers.

"I've made some of my plans," she said, smiling deliciously. "I'm definitely going to suck your cook again."

Spur laughed. "No, I don't mean right now. I mean with your life."

Louella sighed. "I'm trying not to think about that." She bent and, after skidding across the bed, ran her warm tongue along his sensitive, aroused shaft. "I certainly can't stay here." She burrowed a questing finger beneath his balls, pushed in a bit and traced circles around his hairy, dark anus.

McCoy squirmed. "You're not making it easy for me to talk, Louella," Spur said, taking her breasts in his hands and kneading them tenderly.

"You complaining?" Her tongue touched his shaft again as it responded to her ministrations, lenghtening, growing.

"Not exactly," he said, laughing. "You're insatiable, you know that, Louella?"

She smiled. "I guess I am. But is that so bad?"

"Don't talk with your mouth full," Spur said, and flopped back onto the bed.

Louella squealed with delight as she took his length fully.

"But really, Louella, what are your plans?"

The woman slipped the shaft down her throat, then began bobbing her head.

"Are you moving back to Philadelphia to stay with your Aunt Agnes?"

The woman nipped him gently.

"Hey!" he said.

She moved off him and giggled, then began sucking in earnest. This was too much for Spur, so he took her head in his hands, kissed her nose, and pulled her beautiful body up to lay beside him on the bed.

McCoy rolled on top of her and kissed her gently, his tongue tasting, probing. She returned the kiss in earnest, wrapping her legs around his muscled thighs.

When he broke the contact she lifted his right arm and delicately licked the hairs growing there, obviously enjoying his strong, male musk.

"No," she said, pulling her mouth from his salty skin. "I can't go back to Philadelphia," she said. "That hasn't changed—I still hate the city."

"No reason why you should. There's lots of other cities," Spur said, squirming as he caressed her breasts.

"Maybe San Francisco. Or—wherever you're going."

"First I have to send a telegram to my boss—I'll probably do that in San Diego. Next I have to go to San Francisco to deliver the dies to the mint. After that I don't know where I'll be—I never know where my next assignment will take me."

Louella frowned and lifted her head. "Spur McCoy, are you playing hard to get?"

He looked down. "Hard, yes," Spur said. "But not hard to get. It's all yours."

She laughed, then sighed as he plunged into her, connecting their bodies with ten inches of throbbing manhood.

Spur thrust into her now familiar slot, and when he was fully inside her, kissed her again, driving his tongue into her mouth. He repeated the motion with his erection, riding her passionately, then tenderly. He let the animalistic feelings flood through him as her tightness aroused his organ.

"Yes, Spur!" Louella said, then the words were lost as she reached her first orgasm.

Her vagina tightened around him as she shook through her pleasure, sending paroxysms of delight through Spur's nervous system.

"Jesus Christ!" he yelled, and then, with the rickety old bed shaking and Louella twitching and sighing beneath him, Spur screamed and went blind as his lust burst out deep inside her, his hips jerking wildly as he spurt out his seed in an unstoppable flood.

He gasped then and, even before he had recovered from his orgasm, moved within her again. Louella sighed and moved in rhythm with him.

McCoy pumped in earnest as the old-yet-new sensation washed over them again, driving away the horrors of the last night in a sea of sexual bliss.

20

After spending the rest of the morning with
Louella, they had lunch in the hotel kitchen, then
Spur left to see if the town marshal had returned.

He found Weschcke in his office, covered with
dust, and sweating. The man looked up as Spur
entered his office.

"Weschcke," he said in greeting.

"McCoy, you sure were right about Bucher," he
said, shaking his head. "I wouldn't have believed
it if I hadn't seen it with my own eyes."

"What'd you find out there?" Spur took a seat
across from the man's desk.

"The three bodies, as you'd mentioned. I'm
sure you're right—the short one must have been
the one who passed the coins here in town. I've
seen him in town once in a great while. We also
found about 1500 of the counterfeit coins, ready
to be spent. There were also a few more small

bags of free gold hidden in the barn, worth quite a lot of money—maybe two or three pounds worth. There were also thousands more blanks ready to be coated. Then, when I thought I'd found everything, we found two shallow graves on the Bucher ranch. Bad jobs, too.''

Spur whistled. "Was one of them our Indian?"

"Probably. He was a young kid, no more than twenty years old. The other one was an older Indian woman.''

"So that's why Lazy Eye never returned to his camp with Bird Song.''

Weschcke nodded. "If you say so. I'm still wondering about those dies you brought back here—they're perfect. Must've been stolen somewhere along the line, at some time in the past. Bucher bought them and set up his counterfeiting operation here.'' He shook his head. "My bad luck to get the only counterfeiter in the area settled near my town. Make sure you get them safely back to the mint in San Francisco.''

"Right. Did you look to see if Bucher had been mining gold on his property?''

Weschcke nodded. "Yep. Bucher must've spent months cracking rock, but he finally got lucky. It was a small find, but a vein of pure, free gold. All he had to do was melt it down and use it. No smelting, no nothin'.''

"So Louella Bucher will keep the rights to the land, I suppose. And get the gold.''

The town marshal nodded. "After expenses, sure. She'll have to leave me an address before she goes so I can send the money to her."

"I'll tell her. Is that it?" Spur asked.

"Guess so," the man said, nodding. "Christ, I don't know what I would have done without you, McCoy." He looked at Spur gratefully. "I never would've guessed it was Emil Bucher behind all this. You've been a godsend."

"Correction—I've been a government-send."

Weschcke laughed as Spur walked out of his office.

He stopped by his room to find Louella packing and unpacking for her trip, trying to decide what to wear as she decided where to go. He kissed her before riding out on his rented horse to find Bird Song's camp.

McCoy vaguely remembered the instructions the girl had given him and found it without too much trouble.

The Indian woman wasn't beside the dying fire, so Spur tied up his horse and walked down to the stream. He found her sitting on a rock in a small, crudely fenced area.

She looked at him in fright, then relaxed. "You come back."

"Yes."

"Lazy Eye is dead. He has joined my grandfathers." The girl's voice was soft, but it was not a question.

"Yes. I'm sorry."

She nodded. "I knew. I had a vision, but did not understand it until this morning. When the cows disappeared I knew, too, but only in my heart. Now I know up here." She pointed to her head.

Spur was silent.

"I cannot stay here," she said, surveying the surrounding land. "I cannot, but I have nowhere to go." She looked away, then closed her eyes.

"What about your tribe?" Spur asked helpfully. "Can't you go back to your people?"

She frowned. "I have no tribe. Most of them are dead. The rest—all over. I do not know what to do."

Spur had an idea. For some reason he felt responsible for the girl, and couldn't leave Caliente with a clear conscience without trying to help her. "Would you be willing to move your camp? Somewhere else, nearby, where you could work?"

Bird Song cocked her head at him, opening her eyes. "I do not understand."

He thought of Don Guerra. The Mexican might need help on his ranch. "Do you know Don Arturo Guerra's rancho? The friendly Mexican man?"

She thought for a minute, then nodded. "Yes. My brother and I walked beside his camp one day, long ago."

"Maybe you could move your camp nearer to his ranch, and work for him."

She tilted her chin. "Work? What could I do?"

Spur shrugged. "I don't know. Something. I'll ask him to help you."

Sighing, Bird Song rose. "Yes. Please," she said. "I have nothing else, nowhere to go."

"Go to his ranch tomorrow," Spur said softly. "I'm sorry about your brother, Bird Song."

She smiled lightly. "I know."

There was nothing Spur could say.

"At least he is happy now, in the clouds. His spirit has—has *mixed* with the grandfathers and grandmothers, the great spirits. He is at peace."

"Goodbye, Bird Song," Spur said.

"Goodbye, white friend." A tear ran down her cheek. "Thank you for coming back."

Spur walked to his horse and rode leisurely toward *Rancho Hermosa.*

"An Indian Girl?" Arturo Guerra said as he walked with Spur on his ranch an hour later. "Sure, I could use some help. Always need more cooking done, and cleaning. This dust gets everywhere."

Spur smiled. "I'd appreciate it. She should be coming by sometime tomorrow."

"My pleasure—after what you did for Caliente, for the whole area. Yes, I got my miserable cows back, but you brought the man to justice. That is most important."

McCoy heard giggles behind him.

"Spur!"

"*Ai!*" Guerra said.

Lupe and Concha ran up to the two men, lifting their skirts as they came.

"You are back," Lupe said. "Couldn't stay away from us, could you?"

"Lupe, stop it!" Concha said.

Her eyes flashed teasingly. "Do not pretend anymore, sister! You're just jealous that he loves me more than you, Concha! I've known it all the

217

time." Lupe put her arm around Spur's broad shoulders and smiled invitingly up at him. "Isn't that right?" The blonde Mexican girl flapped her lush eyelashes.

"Well, I—" Spur began.

"Muchachas," Guerra said. *"Senor* McCoy is our guest. Do not put him in a difficult situation." His voice was gentle as he lifted Lupe's arm from the man's shoulders. "How could he choose between you?"

"We are getting married," Lupe said, smiling at McCoy. "Isn't that what you whispered into my ear before you left us the other day?"

"Well, I never said—"

"Lupe, behave!" Concha said sternly.

"Jealous!" she hissed and snuggled up beside Spur again. "Go ahead, Concha. Try! You'll never take him away from me!" She grabbed his sides and held on.

"Girls, please!" Guerra said.

Spur laughed. "I don't know what she's talking about," he said, motioning to Lupe.

"Neither do I, most of the time. You understand how it is with young girls, do you not, McCoy?"

He smiled. "Sure."

"All right, Lupe, Concha, leave the man alone. He has to ride back into town."

Lupe frowned. "No. I will not let him! I'll throw my body down on the dust in front of his horse! He'll have to trample me to death to leave!"

Concha took her sister's hand and, with difficulty, pulled her from Spur. "Come on, Lupe.

We have work to do. You have to finish weaving, and I have to start sewing my new dress."

Lupe sighed. "No, Concha! No!"

"Goodbye, Spur," Concha said as she dragged her screaming sister toward the adobe house.

Both men laughed as they went.

Spur found Louella in his hotel room, dressed, her bags packed and piled on the floor.

"You look ready to go somewhere," he said, throwing his hat onto the bed.

"Yes, and you look like you need a bath." She lifted his arm and sniffed, then wrinkled her nose. "You smell like you need one."

Spur laughed. "I love you too, Louella. Anywhere in town I can get one?"

"I asked at the desk downstairs. He just smiled and told me about the river a mile away."

Spur shrugged. "Sounds good to me. Wanna come along?"

She lifted her eyelids. "Spur McCoy, I'm surprised, you asking me a question like that! I wouldn't miss it for the world."

They laughed, got fresh clothing to change into and two towels, then rode the short distance on Spur's horse.

Hot sunlight sparkled on the water's surface as Louella and Spur rode alongside it, searching for a deep pool.

They finally found one and stopped.

"I bet I can get naked before you can," Louella said, tugging at the buttons on her dress.

Spur smiled at the challenge. "Oh yeah?" He

sat, shucked off his boots, then rose to his feet.

Louella dropped her dress and fumbled with her garter belt as Spur let his dirt caked jeans hit the ground, then kicked them off.

They watched each other as they undressed, enjoying the sight of their bodies slowly being revealed. Louella revealed her breasts as she slipped the camisole off over her head, then smiled in appreciation and memory as Spur dropped his shorts at the same second.

"Beat you!" Spur said.

"No you didn't."

He frowned, crossing his arms on his chest. "Okay. Let's call it a tie."

She walked up to him, took his limp penis in her soft hand, and pulled him toward the water.

"Hey!" Spur said, protestingly. "You'll hurt it."

"C'mon, Spur; it's stood up to all the abuse you've been giving it the last twelve hours."

"True."

She laughed and pulled him into the water, where they splashed and washed each other as their bodies slowly adjusted to its icy temperature.

"I'll get ready as soon as we get back to the hotel," Louella said, rubbing water onto his chest, then lifting his arms to wash there. "I want to be all set for tomorrow morning when we take the stagecoach to San Diego." Her voice was bright, cheerful as she smiled at him.

"You in some hurry?" he asked, enjoying her ministrations.

"No. I just didn't want to waste a minute of the rest of the day—or night—doing ridiculous things like packing." Her eyes sparkled.

"I'll go along with that."

"Spur, do you really have to leave me in San Francisco? Can't I come with you?" She nudged him around and slipped her hands over his broad, muscled back.

"I'm sorry, Louella. It's too dangerous. And I never stay in one place for very long. I have too much work to do."

"Then you should take a holiday," she protested, and splashed water between his cheeks, then rubbed her hand between them. He squirmed. "Damnit, Spur, I hate to loose you. You've been the—well, the best thing about this whole trip! What a man you are!" she said, and reached between his legs to grip him.

"Little lady, you talk like that for very long and I might start to listen." He turned around and looked into her eyes.

"Listen. Listen!"

"Nope. Now it's my turn." He slapped down onto the water, completely drenching Louella.

She squealed in delight, her lustrous black hair dripping crystalline drops onto her gleaming, slick body. "Spur McCoy!" she said, gasping. "You bastard!"

"You're a dangerous woman, Louella," he said, standing and rubbing her breasts. "You could make me forget I'm an agent of the Secret Service."

She sighed and smiled as he cupped her breasts.

221

"Okay. But promise me one thing, Spur McCoy."

He looked up at her. "What's that?"

"That you won't leave me until you absolutely have to. Not a minute, not a second before!"

He smiled. It was an easy promise to make.